GHOST WRITER

When Fiona Flint loses her job as a reporter at the Marston Chronicle she becomes a ghost writer, helping senior citizens to publish their memoirs. While interviewing one of her clients, Jason Greaves, she meets his great nephew, Aaron Parker, whom she suspects of trying to defraud elderly investors. Fiona persuades Jeremy Dean, a former colleague, to help her investigate. Jeremy hopes to rekindle their romance, but can she ever forgive the mistake he made in the past?

CATRIONA McCUAIG

GHOST WRITER

Complete and Unabridged

LINFORD
Leicester

First published in Great Britain in 2006

First Linford Edition
published 2007

British Library CIP Data

McCuaig, Catriona
    Ghost writer.—Large print ed.—
    Linford romance library
    1. Love stories
    2. Large type books
    I. Title
    823.9′2 [F]

    ISBN 978–1–84617–872–6

Published by
F. A. Thorpe (Publishing)
Anstey, Leicestershire

Set by Words & Graphics Ltd.
Anstey, Leicestershire
Printed and bound in Great Britain by
T. J. International Ltd., Padstow, Cornwall

This book is printed on acid-free paper

1

It was a glorious May morning. Poets may write about wanting to be in England when April's there, but as far as Fiona Flint was concerned there was nothing to beat May, with flowers blooming and all the birds singing. In fact, her heart was singing, too, and why not? She had a job she loved, and a man with whom she was on the brink of falling in love, so what more could any girl ask of life?

She'd been a reporter on the Marston Chronicle for two years now, and was well aware of her luck in landing a job in her home town. Not only could she live at home, where her contribution to the household income was far less than if she had a flat of her own, but she knew the area and its people like the back of her hand, which was a distinct asset in her work. And the recent arrival on the team was just the icing on the cake. Jeremy Dean, tall, good looking and athletic, had lost no time in inviting her out, and now everyone regarded them as an item.

'What's going on in there?' she asked, nodding in the direction of Mr Kemp's office. It was unusual for the editor's door to be closed this early on a Monday morning. Usually he was striding about, giving out assignments for the week and bawling at people whose work was late reaching his desk.

'Don't ask me, I'm only the assistant sales person!' Cherry Stenhouse shrugged. 'The door was closed when I got here. Maybe he's brought his breakfast to work with him and doesn't want anyone to know he didn't have time to eat before he left home.'

Fiona booted up her computer and stared moodily at the unfinished assignment which came up on her desktop. She had been sent to cover a fashion show featuring the work of an up-and-coming young designer, and she was having trouble producing a review which was both truthful and yet not totally unkind.

His stuff was so horrible that she wondered if the man had some deep seated grudge against women. She couldn't imagine anyone wanting to wear such ghastly creations, let alone pay out good money to buy them. The worst of it was that the designer, Damon Frew, was the grandson of one of their major advertisers and there would be big trouble if she panned the collection completely. She sighed. Perhaps a cup of strong black coffee would help her to collect her thoughts.

The editor's door flew open and Jeremy Dean stalked out, head down. He went to his desk without casting a glance in her direction, which was odd, after the wonderful day they'd had on the river yesterday. Perhaps Mr Kemp had given him a rocket for some reason? She wasn't left in ignorance for long. The editor appeared in the doorway.

'Can I have a word, Fee?'

What could she have done? Nothing, as far as she knew. All last week's work had been completed well before the deadline, and a reader had actually written in to praise one of her recent pieces. She took a deep breath and went into the lion's den, unaware that Jeremy was watching her with a troubled look in his eyes.

'Shut the door, Fee, and come and sit down.' The editor rubbed his hand over his mouth as if trying to find the right words to express what he was thinking, which was highly unusual for him. He cleared his throat. 'You've heard about the proposed takeover, Fee?'

'Yes, we're being bought out by the Rufus Filey chain.'

'Exactly. Well, it's gone through, and I've just received a directive from the top brass telling me that as a result there has to be some streamlining at the grass roots level.'

Puzzled, Fiona waited. Mr Kemp

4

cleared his throat again.

'Yes, well. Downsizing, call it what you like. The point is, there has to be a redundancy and I have to lay off one of my reporters.'

So that was it. Poor Jeremy. He'd only joined them two months ago, so pleased to have this chance after being out of work for some time, and now he was jobless again.

'So I'm very sorry, Fee, but there it is. I'll give you a good reference, of course, you've worked well here and been an asset to us.'

'What!' Fiona came to in a hurry. 'You're telling me I'm sacked?'

'Oh, let's not use that word,' he protested. 'You're not being fired. There is a difference, you know.' Trust him to start up a discussion on the meaning of words!

'Why me, and not Jeremy, Mr Kemp? Whatever happened to last in, first out?'

'I had to look at this from all angles. Dean has an excellent background in sports reporting, a department which the owners are keen to see us expand here.'

'So? I can cover cricket matches and football games. I always did before he came here, and you know that.'

'You're a woman, Fee, and that means you can't go into the changing rooms after a match. And, as Dean says, that's where the good stories are often found, in the chit chat immediately afterwards.'

Fiona couldn't believe her ears. 'Jeremy said that? You mean when you called him in here to sack him he managed to talk you into changing your mind?'

The editor turned pink around the ears. 'Not exactly. He put it to me before I had a chance to say anything, but I admit it does make sense. I'm sorry, Fee, but there it is.'

He quailed under her disgusted look. 'It could be worse,' he mumbled. 'They're giving you a month's pay in lieu of notice, so you can go today if you want to.'

Banging the door behind her she stormed over to Jeremy's desk. He flinched under her furious gaze but she felt no sympathy for him.

'You rat, Jeremy Dean! I thought you cared about me, but only a complete rotter could do a thing like this. You knew there were going to be redundancies, so you took good care that I was to be out on my ear instead of you. Oh, I could just kill you!'

'I'm sorry,' he muttered. 'I wasn't trying to do anything at your expense. I just needed to prove that I'm indispensable. You know I was out of work for a long time before I came here. I have debts, Fiona. I can't afford to be on the dole again. Anyway, it wasn't necessarily you who'd lose out. I thought they might get Beaver to take early retirement.'

'Beaver!' she huffed, glaring in the direction of Ben Hudson who had been with the paper since he'd left school at the age of fifteen. 'The only way he'll leave early is if he drops dead, you know that.'

Jeremy spread his hands wide. 'What can I say? You win some, you lose some, that's life.'

'I'll never speak to you again, Jeremy Dean!' she snarled. 'And you can write that beastly fashion story. My notes are on my desk.'

'Me, write about women's fashions?' he bleated, horrified. 'I don't have a clue!'

'Tough!' she barked, turning her back on him and making what she hoped was a dignified exit.

Cherry, who had been listening to this exchange in growing dismay, followed her friend into the loo where she found Fiona in floods of tears.

'It's just not fair,' she hiccupped, wiping her eyes on the sleeve of her sweat shirt.

'Perhaps you can sue them for wrongful dismissal,' Cherry suggested.

'I doubt it. Redundancies happen all the time. Anyway, if I did get my job back I couldn't possibly work here after that. I'm not thick-skinned enough.'

'I suppose not,' Cherry murmured. 'You might get a settlement, though.'

But Fiona shook her head. All she wanted was to forget about this place once and for all, and never come near it again. As for Jeremy Dean, she was going to pretend that he'd never existed.

★   ★   ★

'Home so early? There's nothing wrong, is there?' Madge Flint mumbled through the clothes peg she was holding between her lips as she fastened a billowing sheet to the line. Fiona helped her to clamp it down before the stiff breeze tore it away from them.

'You could say that, Mum! I've only lost my job, and my boyfriend as well!'

'Oh, dear. Run in and put the kettle on, then. I'll be with you in a minute.' Madge was not the type to fly apart at the first hint of trouble. In one way Fiona could have used a mother who enfolded her in a hug and encouraged her to sob out her troubles, but on

9

the other hand perhaps the practical approach was more useful.

Fiona poured out her sad story, placing great emphasis on her feelings about Jeremy's betrayal.

'Oh, well, plenty more fish in the sea,' her mother said comfortably. 'That goes for jobs as well as boyfriends! I know it's a shock, being laid off without warning, but if you get no worse in life, my girl, you'll do all right. As for that Jeremy, isn't it just as well you found out now what he's like, before you got too closely involved?'

Put like that it made sense, but it didn't take away the pain. And Jeremy had seemed so nice. Would she ever be able to trust a man again? Maybe they were all tarred with the same brush, she thought, blinking back her tears.

'You know what they say about getting back on a horse right after you've fallen off,' Madge continued. 'That's what you should do. Go out and find another job right away, before you lose confidence.'

2

Despite her mother's calm assurance, Fiona quickly learned that finding another job was easier said than done. She decided against going to the job centre, where posts in journalism were unlikely to be listed. Nor did she spend much time looking in the *Situations Vacant* in the newspapers, which her mother didn't quite understand.

'None of the jobs I've seen advertised are what I want, Mum.'

'Surely it's a case of any port in a storm, Fiona? Take what you can get while you're waiting for the ideal job to come up.'

'What I was doing at The Chronicle was my ideal job. I'm not ruthless enough to work on a big daily, and I could never survive on one of those awful tabloids. I just don't like hurting people's feelings.'

'So what are you going to do, then?'

'Jobs that are going on a weekly paper are usually advertised in their own pages, which I wouldn't be likely to see. So I'm going to blanket all the weeklies in the south with my resumé, asking them to keep it on file until something comes up, if they have nothing to offer at present. Meanwhile, I'll drop in to see the editor of The Marston News. I'm a good reporter and he must know my work. When his paper comes out we all skim through it at once, to see if he's managed to scoop us on anything, and I'm sure he does the same with The Chronicle.'

Madge noticed that her daughter was speaking in the present tense, as if she was still part of The Chronicle team, but wisely she held her tongue. 'Good thinking,' she murmured. 'It would be one in the eye for that lot if you get taken on by The News.'

Unfortunately, that didn't work out as the pair of them had hoped. Fiona stepped into the office of the rival paper, her appearance heralded by the jangling of the old-fashioned bell over the door. The News was one of the few remaining weeklies in the area that was still under private ownership, most having been absorbed into the larger chains.

The publisher and editor was Crispin Tighe, a newspaperman of the old school. While he had updated his operation to keep up with modern technology he himself looked like something out of an old movie, with his green eye shade and elastic arm bands. Fiona suspected that this was done for effect.

'I heard you were let go from that place,' he sniffed, looking her up and down in an insulting manner. 'And I suppose you've come here looking for a job.'

Fiona straightened her shoulders. 'Yes, please.' She opened her bag and fumbled for her resumé, which he added to the pile of paper on his desk without looking at it.

'We've nothing to offer at present, but there will be an opening next month when one of my reporters goes on maternity leave. Maternity leave!' He looked as if he wanted to spit. 'There was none of that nonsense when I started out. That's all very fine for big companies with money to burn, but it wreaks havoc on small places like this. I'd prefer to hire men only, if the equality police would allow it, but can I get my hands on them? No! All the young fellows head straight for the big dailies.'

Except for the likes of Jeremy Dean, Fiona thought, bitterness welling up inside her. She didn't think much of Mr Tighe's attitude towards women, either, but if she wanted a job she had to keep her opinion to herself.

Tighe fumbled through the papers on his desk and produced a letter which he waved triumphantly under her nose. 'This is from a young lassie who's just finished college. She wants to come here and work for nothing, d'you see?'

14

Fiona nodded. This was becoming quite normal nowadays. Caught in a bind, unable to land a job because employers favoured applicants with experience, young graduates tried to get a foot in the door by offering their services for free. Fine for those who could afford it, but not so good for those who needed an income so they could start to pay off their debts.

'I was going to phone and tell her to come ahead,' Tighe nodded, 'but now you're here I suppose I could give you a chance. How would you feel about working here for a few months on the same basis, until we see how it pans out?' He tilted his chair back, peering up at her from under his visor, with a half smile on his face.

'You mean, you want me to work here for nothing?' Fiona spluttered, unable to believe what she was hearing. 'I'm an experienced reporter, Mr Tighe, and a good one, too, if I do say so myself. The labourer is worthy of her hire, sir!'

'An experienced reporter without a job,' he reminded her. 'Let's say you come here for a month at your own expense, and if I'm satisfied, then I'll keep you on and pay you our starting rate. What do you think of that?'

'Not much!' she snapped, and turned on her heel and left in a hurry. She seemed to be making a habit of storming out of editors' offices these days. Outside in the street she found that she was shaking, although whether this was a result of nerves or anger she would have been hard put to it to explain.

'I should jolly well think so!' her mother retorted when she heard how Fiona had stamped out of the office. 'The cheek of the man! Who does he think he is?'

'Someone who holds all the cards,' Fiona said sadly. 'I suppose I can't blame him, really. If he can get an eager young college grad free of charge, why shouldn't he take advantage of the situation?'

★ ★ ★

Several weeks went by, during which Fiona learned to dread the arrival of the postman with the neatly self-addressed stamped envelopes she had included with her applications.

The letters inside all said more or less the same thing. Nothing available in the foreseeable future. We wish you luck in finding a suitable post.

'I bet they all have youngsters looking for work experience,' she said gloomily. 'Nothing at all for people who really know what they're doing.'

'Never mind, dear,' Madge said. 'Something will turn up eventually, you'll see.'

What did turn up was a letter from her mother's aunt in Canada.

'This looks interesting,' Madge remarked, handing a booklet to Fiona while refer- ring to the letter which had accompanied it. 'Auntie Freda says she's had her life story recorded by a sort of ghost writer who came and interviewed her at her home, and then had it made up into books for giving out to family members. Quite a good idea, really.

'Freda met her husband during the war when he was over here with the Canadian army. When it was all over she was one of the youngest war brides to go over there to join him.'

Fiona turned the little book over in her hand. It consisted of four dozen pages of type and photos, and was written in the first person, 'as told to' a Joanna Burke. Yes, it certainly was a good idea.

As an ordinary person Freda hadn't lived the sort of life which had fitted her to write an autobiography which would appear in the shops but her memoir was certainly of interest to her nearest and dearest.

'I could do this, Mum! I wouldn't get rich doing it, but if I could get enough customers the money would tide me over until I get another job. What do you think?'

'You're certainly qualified for it, dear,

after working as a newspaper reporter.'

'And the finished products will be a nice addition to my book of clippings when I go for job interviews.'

Feeling more cheerful than she had been since losing her job at The Chronicle, Fiona set to work at once to prepare an advertisement for the newspaper.

'Record your life story now, to share with family and friends! Experienced reporter will interview you in your home and edit your words for publication. Reasonable rates.'

She then visited a firm which printed copies on demand to find out about their charges for a limited number of books. This sum, added to a modest fee for her own work of interviewing clients, making up the pages on her computer and scanning in the photos, would make up the final cost.

At her mother's suggestion she also drew up a contract for the clients to sign. Madge also advised her to ask for a deposit as a sign of good faith. All

Fiona had to do now was to cross her fingers and wait for the public to beat a path to her door.

In the week following publication of her advertisement she was delighted to receive four phone calls. One was from a Mr Jason Greaves who expressed a definite interest, another was from a woman who wanted Fiona to 'call round to discuss the matter' and two more were from enquirers who hung up without committing themselves after hearing what the project would cost. Fiona made appointments to meet the first two callers and felt she was off to a good start.

'I've always wanted to do something like this,' Mr Greaves told her, 'but somehow I've never got around to it. Now you've come along I just might manage it.'

She took an immediate liking to the elderly man and knew she'd enjoy working with him. She was a bit taken aback on learning that he had no children to share the finished book with, but he assured her that he had plenty of old pals at the Golden Age Club who would love to have a copy.

'And when they see them, perhaps you'll get a few more clients,' he enthused.

She fared less well when she called on Mrs Allen, who turned out to be a large woman, weighed down with masses of costume jewellery. After spending ten minutes boasting about the interesting life she'd led, the blow fell.

'Of course, your charges are much too high, my dear! I said to my hubby, I said, someone is making a fat profit! And he said I should speak to you about it, get you to take something off the top, especially when I'm one of your first clients, why, with my contacts, I can get you oodles of work if you do a decent enough job!'

Fiona felt her temper rising, but she strove to remain pleasant. 'I'm sorry, Mrs Allen. The price stands. I have no control over the cost of printing, which makes up the greater part of the amount. I have to get something for my time and effort, or there would be no point in doing this at all. I do hope you understand.'

'It's your loss, then, Miss Flint! I did think you might meet me half way on this. My hubby was sure that you would.'

Privately Fiona decided that hubby would probably say anything for a quiet life, but she merely ended the conversation as pleasantly as she could, and took her leave. She only hoped that the woman wouldn't gossip to her cronies and cause her to lose potential customers.

'How did it go, dear?' Madge Flint was genuinely interested and had already decided to have her own life story recorded, on a paying basis.

'One up, one down, Mum. Mr Greaves is a real pet, but that Mrs Allen only wanted to beat me down on the price. I hope they're not all like that!'

Just then the phone rang. The caller

was a Mrs Myrtle Siddons.

'I phoned earlier, dear, to ask about the cost. I've decided I can just manage it, so can we go ahead with it, please? I think you'll enjoy hearing my story. I was an evacuee during the war, you know. I came from St Albans and there were some dreadful air raids around there, which was why my parents decided to let me be sent away.'

'I'd be delighted to work with you on that,' Fiona told her. 'We could get started right away, if you're free tomorrow?'

'That is good news, dear,' Madge said, when she saw her daughter's glowing face. 'Two clients already, and three if you count me. Won't Auntie Freda be surprised when I send her my little book in exchange for her own!'

'And I owe her a vote of thanks for giving me the idea.' Fiona smiled.

3

Jason Greaves lived in a small house on a quiet street. Every room — at least, those which Fiona was allowed to see — was crammed with memorabilia, ranging from small silver trophies to photographs of men in sports gear.

'You must have lived here a long time,' she marvelled, thinking that if he ever moved away a very large truck would be needed to transport that lot.

'Born and bred in this house,' he said proudly, causing her heart to sink. How was she supposed to make his life sound exciting if he had never been farther than Marston?

Perhaps she could make something of his sports activities, although even the matches played at the local level were hardly stop-press news. That did give her an idea, though; she could look through back issues of The Chronicle and perhaps dig up some mention of his past triumphs.

'You've lived here all your life, then,' she said.

'Except when I was serving in France, during the war, of course.'

'You don't look old enough!' She smiled, only partly in flattery because Mr Greaves looked quite distinguished with his intense blue eyes, white hair and firm jaw line.

'I'm not, either! Lied about my age, didn't I! Just sixteen when I joined up, silly young fool. Wanted to get involved while there was still time, afraid it would all come to an end before I got the chance to get into the scrap. Then I found myself on the Normandy beaches on D-Day and wished I'd stayed home where I belonged!'

This was more like it, the angle she was looking for. 'Do you have any photographs I could look at, Mr Greaves? We need to select a few to include in your book.'

'Plenty in those albums over there,'

he nodded, indicating a book shelf bulging with well-thumbed volumes. 'And I definitely want to use that one of my late wife, Muriel.' He pointed to a picture in a silver frame, that held pride of place on the mantelpiece.

They were deeply engrossed in their work when a tall figure loomed in the doorway, making Fiona jump. She hadn't heard anyone come in, and was rather alarmed by the man's sudden appearance. Mr Greaves looked up in annoyance.

'Aaron! This is a private house, you know. Don't you ever knock? And what do you want this time?'

'What sort of greeting is that, Uncle? Anyway, if you want to keep people out, you should lock your doors. I've told you that often enough, haven't I? And who might this lovely young lady be? Aren't you going to introduce us?' He grinned at Fiona, showing perfect white teeth.

Mr Greaves' only response was a grunt, as he continued to riffle through his large selection of snaps. Fiona thrust out her hand.

'How do you do? I'm Fiona Flint.'

'Aaron Parker, Jason's nephew. Are you the daily help?'

Fiona bristled. Not that there was anything wrong with helping elderly people with their housework, far from it. It was just that she was proud of her training as a reporter and liked to have her achievements recognised.

'I'm helping Mr Greaves to record his life story. As you can see, we're trying to choose the photos to be included in the book.'

'There had better be one of me, then, as I'm the old boy's favourite nephew!' He laughed.

Mr Greaves muttered something under his breath that Fiona couldn't quite catch, but she guessed it wasn't complimentary.

'Anyway, I'm sorry to interrupt this cosy chat, but I've come a long way to speak to Uncle on business, so perhaps you can deal with this another day?'

'Certainly.' Annoyed at this cursory dismissal, Fiona got to her feet. 'I'll see you tomorrow, then, Mr Greaves, all right? I can see myself out.'

As she closed the front door behind her she heard what sounded like an argument breaking out. Aaron was speaking firmly, overriding Mr Greaves' querulous tones.

Well, it wasn't her business, and she could use the rest of the morning to search through the old files of The Chronicle, which were on microfilm at the public library. She was glad that she didn't have to visit the newspaper office to do that!

After lunch she called on Mrs Siddons, who seemed delighted to see her.

'Come on in, dear. I was just making tea. I'm sure you'll join me in a cup?'

'Yes, thank you, Mrs Siddons.'

'Oh, do call me Myrtle. Everyone does! I can't wait to get started on my book, not that I served as an international spy, or anything exciting like that.

My daughter says she's looking forward to getting hold of a copy to find out if I've spilled all the family secrets!'

Fiona took an instant liking to the bubbly, grey-haired Myrtle, with her sparkling eyes and trim figure. She decided that the ideal place to start was with her experience as a wartime evacuee, perhaps discussing the shock of being taken from a happy family to move in with complete strangers. However, unlike some poor children that Fiona had read about, Myrtle's experience had been positive.

'I missed my parents very much, of course, and worried about what might be happening to them, but the people who took me in were kind. Very kind indeed. A Mr and Mrs Wilmott. Uncle Jack and Auntie Rene, I called them, though they were no relation. It was because of the happy times I had with them that I decided to come back to Marston after my husband died. The house was far too big for one person, so I decided that a complete break was on the cards. I've been here three months now. Of course, the Wilmotts are long dead, so I don't know many folks here yet.'

'You were evacuated to Marston!'

'Why, yes, dear, didn't I say? I lived on Flynn Street and attended the local school just around the corner.'

'What a coincidence. I have another client who lives on Flynn Street, a Mr Greaves.'

Myrtle's jaw dropped. 'But they lived next door to us! Who is it, Jason or Jack?'

'Jason,' Fiona told her, and was enchanted to see a dreamy expression cross the older woman's still pretty face.

'Well I never did! To think that Jason is still here, after all these years!'

'You must have known him well, then.'

'My dear, we were childhood sweethearts!'

'And then you were separated by the war and never saw each other again,'

Fiona said, sensing romance and already making plans to reunite the star-crossed lovers.

Myrtle laughed. 'In a way, I suppose we were, though we were much too young at the time for it to have come to anything. I was only fourteen and Jason two years older. We did exchange a couple of inept kisses, as I recall, but there wasn't much more to it than that.

'I suffered through the agonies of first love when Jason ran off to fight Hitler, as he put it, but eventually I went back to St Albans and picked up the threads of my life there. I forgot all about him when I met Stan — that was my late husband — and the pair of us had many happy years together, bringing up a family.'

Later that day Madge Flint was intrigued to hear about the amazing coincidence of Fiona's two clients having been friends so long ago. 'I hope you're not thinking of match-making, though,' she warned. 'That could lead to trouble.'

'Don't be silly, Mum! They're both fast approaching eighty! I do think they might enjoy a get-together, though, and that will help me, if I can get them talking about the good old days. They'll be able to jog each other's memories.'

'You bring them here, then, and I'll do a nice tea for them.' Madge's eyes were gleaming and Fiona knew that her mother was just as keen as she was to see what might happen next. Laughing, she agreed to issue the invitation.

★　★　★

Fiona experienced a sudden shock when she came face to face with Jeremy as she dashed out of the bakery, clutching a cottage loaf and a box of cream doughnuts. The unwrapped loaf flew out of her hands and would have landed in the rain-filled gutter had it not been for a magnificent save on his part.

'That was a close one,' he panted, handing over the bread as he stepped back on to the pavement.

'Yes, thank you,' she said stiffly, preparing to make a dignified retreat.

'Hey, hold on a minute!' he said. 'Do you have time for a coffee or something? I want to hear all your news.'

'I don't have any particular news. Now, if you'll excuse me, I must get on.'

'But I really do want to know how things are with you,' he pleaded. 'Cherry told me you've gone freelance and I wondered how that's going.'

'Did she, now! Well, for your information, things are going very well indeed.'

'Then I suppose you've got yourself listed with the National Union of Journalists' freelance directory?'

'No, I haven't actually.'

'Oh, but you should. They're online now, you know.'

Fiona was incensed. 'When I want your advice, Jeremy Dean, I'll ask for it!' She stepped around him and stalked off, her high heels clattering.

'But I only wanted to help!' he bawled, but she wasn't interested in what he had to say. It was bad enough that he'd done her out of a perfectly good job, without trying to tell her how to conduct her life as well.

Of course, she thought glumly, it had been a lie to say that her working life was going well. She just didn't want to give him the satisfaction of knowing that things were as rocky as they were. She certainly hoped that her ghost writing business would take off, but that would take time, and if it wasn't for Mum she wouldn't even have a roof over her head once her severance pay ran out.

She decided to walk home to save on bus fare, having given up driving her car for the duration. Her resentful thoughts kept her going and it wasn't until she turned in at the gate that she realised she had reached the house. Unfortunately she had also realised something else, and that was that she still had strong feelings for the rat.

'How is that possible?' she demanded of the cat, who had got up from the doorstep and come forward to greet her. 'It's utterly stupid to keep loving someone who is totally undeserving. I'm an idiot, that's what it is!'

'Talking to yourself, dear?'

'Oh, hello Mum. I didn't see you there.' Madge Flint had come round the side of the house with a hand-fork and a trug in her hands. 'No, I was speaking to Henry, who was no help at all!' Henry arched his back and rubbed against her legs.

'Something wrong, is there?'

'Not really. I bumped into Jeremy in the High Street and we had words.'

'Oh, him! Never mind, as soon as I get this border seen to we'll make an attack on whatever it is you have in that box. I could do with a pick-me-up myself.'

Henry followed Fiona into the house, looking hopeful. She filled his dish with dry cat food, which he regarded with disgust. 'It's that or nothing, my lad.

You know what the vet said. You're in danger of getting a fatty heart.'

And that will be my problem next, she reflected, as she opened the box of doughnuts and put two of them on a plate. She had just finished reading a magazine article in which two women had successfully slimmed down after being obese for several years. In both cases they had began to overeat after losing their jobs and being dumped by their partners.

'I'm not letting you do that to me, Jeremy Dean!' she vowed.

4

The more she saw of Myrtle Siddons, the more Fiona liked her. She was full of fun and when anything went wrong on the domestic front she always managed to look on the bright side.

'That's what brought us through the war, you see.' She nodded when Fiona commented on her positive attitude to life. 'That was Hitler's plan, you know, when he sent his Luftwaffe over to bomb our cities. He wanted to destroy our morale so we'd give up easily when the invasion came, but it didn't work. No matter what happened, people just held their heads high and carried on regardless.'

'That must have been so hard to do when people lost their homes or their loved ones,' Fiona murmured.

'Of course it was, dear, but that's life. When bad things happen you just have to keep going, don't you?'

Fiona digested this thought while her new-found friend was putting the kettle on. When she herself had lost both her job and her boyfriend it would have been easy enough to wallow in misery but instead she was on the verge of an interesting new career. Perhaps there was some of that good old wartime British steel in her make-up after all!

'Now, where was I?' Myrtle said, when she had settled down again with a cup of steaming tea in one hand and a Bourbon biscuit in the other. 'Yes, I was telling you about being evacuated to Marston, that's right. As I understand it now, the government were making plans to send children away from the big cities, even before war was declared. It was all very well for that Mr Chamberlain to talk about peace in our time and all that, but some people could see the writing on the wall, believe you me.'

'So you came to Marston as soon as war was declared?'

'Oh, no, dear. At first my parents didn't want to let me go at all. Mum kept saying that if that man was going to drop bombs on us, then we'd all go together. What if they let me go among strangers and then got killed themselves? Where would I end up?

'A lot of children did go, and then nothing much happened for months, and they all came back. It was only after the London blitz started in 1941 that things got moving again, and that's when I arrived here.'

'So your mother changed her mind, then.'

'It was Dad, actually. He said that if all those Nasties landed and started killing, I'd be safer here. That's what he called them, he meant Nazis, of course, but nasty is just what they were.

'Of course, I didn't want to go away, but in those days we obeyed our parents unless we wanted a good clip round the ear, so I got on the train with the rest of them, with a label on my coat, and was posted off like a blooming parcel.'

'And the next thing was, you met the Greaves brothers!' Fiona teased.

'Not right away, dear. I did find myself living right next door to them, but we didn't think much of each other at first. They were at the age when they still thought that girls were soppy, and I thought they were a couple of rough customers because they were always pushing and jostling and kicking that football of theirs about. Later of course, it was a different story.' She smiled reminiscently.

'So how did it feel when you met Jason again after all these years?' Fiona was hoping for some emotionally charged feelings to add to the drama, but she was to be disappointed. Myrtle waved her hands dramatically.

'My dear, I haven't seen the man again to this day! I wouldn't have known he was still alive if you hadn't mentioned it.'

'But surely you wondered about him? Surely returning to Marston has stirred up old memories!'

40

'Old memories, yes, but in my mind Jason is still the teenager I knew, who bravely went off to war before he was old enough to be called up. Don't forget that I went back to St Albans before he returned home. A lot of water has gone under the bridge since then, Fiona. Sixty years' worth, in fact! I know what people say about how you never forget your first love, but when you've been married to someone else for many years and raised a family, all those memories are much more important.'

'So you're not the tiniest bit curious, then?' Fiona asked slyly.

Myrtle blushed. 'Now, I didn't say that! I'm looking forward to this little tea that your mother is so kindly getting up for us and as long as Jason doesn't bore us with his war reminiscences it should be most enjoyable.'

'I'll see that he doesn't,' Fiona said. 'I shall tell him he must keep those for his book. Anyway, I expect he's thrilled with the idea of meeting you again and will want to know what you've been doing all these years.'

If Jason Greaves was thrilled at the idea of having tea at the Flint home, he had a funny way of showing it. He looked at Fiona blankly when she issued the invitation.

'How old is your mother?' he demanded.

'What?' She was taken aback by this rude response. What on earth had that to do with anything?

'Your mother, Miss Flint. I think you've told me she's a widow, but to judge from the look of you, she can't be all that old.'

'She's not,' Fiona told him. Madge was in her fifties and liked to keep quiet about it. She would have shot her daughter if that fact was broadcast in the town!

Now it was his turn to be puzzled. 'Look, Mr Greaves,' Fiona said, trying to interpret his expression, 'I think there may have been some sort of misunderstanding. My mother loves to entertain, and she'd like to meet my clients, that's all. I don't quite see what bearing her age has on that.'

'So it won't be just the two of us there, then?'

'Of course not. I'll be there, and so will another of my clients.'

'Oh, dear. I'm afraid I may have jumped to the wrong conclusion.'

Poor Mr Greaves was pink with embarrassment. 'It's just that ever since my dear wife passed away, I've been inundated with invitations to tea from older women of all shapes and sizes. One even went so far as to call me 'an eligible widower' to my face! I um, er . . .'

His voice trailed off and Fiona had to hide a smirk. 'So you naturally assumed that my mother was one of the 'monstrous regiment.''

'I'm afraid so.'

'Then let's start again from the beginning. Will you accept Mum's invitation?'

'Certainly. I'll be most delighted.'

Later, Madge howled with laughter when she heard this story. 'Imagine me, a femme fatale! I can't wait to meet the old boy. He must be really something if all those old gals are after him like wasps around the jam pot.'

'He is quite attractive for his age,' Fiona admitted, 'but I think it has more to do with there being so few widowers in that age group for lonely old ladies to latch on to. Added to which, I think he may be quite well off. Not that he's mentioned that sort of thing, but he has some lovely antiques in his house as well as some expensive-looking paintings.'

'Which could, of course, have been handed down in his family. Oh well, as long as he knows I'm not after his money, it should turn out to be an interesting afternoon.'

'Unless he runs a mile when he sees our Myrtle, thinking she's after him as well,' Fiona mused. 'I'm beginning to think that this get-together wasn't such a great idea after all, Mum.'

'Nonsense! Just you leave everything to me,' Madge said firmly.

Fiona need not have worried. Myrtle and Jason greeted each other with cries of amazement.

'Imagine that' and 'who would have thought it' were expressions heard more than once as Madge passed the cucumber sandwiches and dispensed endless cups of tea.

'And what about Jack? What's become of him?' Myrtle said at last, neatly heading off Jason's foray into what happened on D-Day, following his explanation to Fiona's mother that he hadn't seen Myrtle since then.

'He died two years ago,' Jason told her. A stroke. Never did take care of himself, did our Jack.'

'I'm sorry,' she murmured. 'So you have no living relatives, now?'

'There's Rita, Jack's daughter. I never see anything of her. She lives in

Southampton with her second husband.'

'What about Aaron Parker, then? The man I met at your house, Mr Greaves?'

Jason glared at Fiona. 'Oh, him! That's Rita's son. Calls himself my nephew, but of course he's not. Great nephew is the term, I believe, although that's a misnomer if ever there was one. Nothing great about Aaron Parker, I can tell you that!'

There was an uncomfortable silence, which Madge filled by asking if anyone would like more cake. Fiona sensed a mystery here, and she vowed to get to the bottom of her client's dislike of young Mr Parker, if she could think of a diplomatic way of doing so. It might add spice to the story.

Myrtle Siddons caught her eye and winked. Obviously she was enjoying her reunion with her old friend, and Fiona realised that it might be useful to pump her for stories about the Greaves family.

She obviously must have known Jack,

all those years ago, and what she had to say about him would help to round out Jason's background.

He had been athletic and daring enough to join up to serve his country at a very young age. Had Jack been like that too, or had the two brothers been completely different. Perhaps they had each inherited their talents from older family members.

'This has been quite delightful, Mrs Flint,' Jason was saying now. 'You must allow me to return your kind hospitality some day soon. I don't entertain at home any more now that my dear wife is no longer with me, but I do enjoy an evening out at a good restaurant. Of course, I mean all three of you,' he added, as Myrtle's face fell. Shall we set a date soon?'

* * *

'I must say this is much better than I expected! Your Jeremy seems to be a man of many talents! I'm surprised

47

he even knows about such things as chiffon and butter muslin, not to mention camisole tops and sweetheart necklines.'

Madge had unearthed the previous week's crumpled copy of The Chronicle from behind one of the sofa cushions and was scanning the fashion story on one of the inside pages. 'I suppose you didn't mean me to see this, so you hid it where you thought I wouldn't find it.'

'No, I put it there as a test, to see how often you clean the furniture,' Fiona snapped, immediately regretting her sarcasm. 'I'm sorry, Mum. I didn't mean to jump down your throat. And of course, he doesn't know a polo neck from a polo pony! He had a perfectly good set of notes to work from, based on my very careful summary of what was on offer at the fashion show, and now that I'm gone he's taking all the credit for my work.'

'Then you should have destroyed those notes before you left the office,' her mother said loyally. But Fiona had been too professional for that. If her review of the collection had failed to get into print it was the young designer who would have suffered, not Jeremy Dean.

Madge was a great believer in giving people enough rope to hang themselves. 'Never mind, dear. I expect he'll fall flat on his face one of these days and then you'll have the last laugh.' Somehow that thought did little to comfort her daughter.

Fiona dodged into the doorway of Boots to avoid being seen by Jeremy Dean. Cherry Stenhouse was with him, teetering along on three-inch heels with a long expanse of leg showing beneath her brief skirt.

She looked daggers at their retreating backs. Cherry was supposed to be a friend. How could she? Reason took over; there was no longer anything between Fiona and Jeremy so he could date whom ever he liked, and the same went for Cherry. Anyway, it might not

49

be a date at all. Colleagues often went for coffee or a meal together without there being anything more to it than that. All the same, this had come as a shock.

'Are you waiting for someone?'

Fiona came to with a start, looking up at the man who had spoken.

'Oh, hello. Mr Parker, isn't it?'

'Aaron, please.'

'Aaron, then.'

'I was just on my way to the Copper Kettle for a coffee. Care to join me?'

Fiona hesitated. From what she had seen when Aaron had called at Mr Greaves' house she didn't care for him all that much, but what harm could there be in having coffee with him?

She might learn something about his family background to include in the book, and a spiteful little voice in her head whispered that it wouldn't hurt for Jeremy to see her with a presentable looking man. It would be evidence that she wasn't losing any sleep over Jeremy Dean!

'Thanks, I could do with something myself.' She smiled, trying not to show her distaste when Aaron took her by the elbow and steered her in the direction recently taken by the pair from The Chronicle.

When they got inside she pretended not to notice the other pair, but Cherry sighted her at once and gave a cheerful wave. Fiona waved back, studiously avoiding looking in Jeremy's direction.

Her plan was to put on an animated performance, laughing and talking to show how little she cared, but there was little opportunity to try out her acting skills since Aaron spent most of the time talking about himself.

She gathered that he was some sort of top-flight financial consultant, but she wasn't sure what was meant by that. Presumably he helped people to invest their money, taking a percentage when things went well, but how that was different from being a bank manager or a stockbroker she had no idea.

Cherry and Jeremy got up and left. Watching them go, Fiona suddenly realised that Aaron had asked her a question and was actually waiting for an answer.

'Oh, sorry. I just noticed some friends of mine and didn't catch what you were saying.'

'I said, I wondered how much spare change Uncle Jason has lying around, that's all.'

'Spare change? Coins, do you mean, for tipping the paper boy or something?'

'Come now, Fiona, you know that's not what I meant. How much is the old boy worth? Does he keep it in an old sock under the mattress, or is it in savings bonds or something?'

'I really have no idea!' she said stiffly. 'We talk about his wartime experiences, and his involvement in sports when he was younger. Anything more personal is none of my business, is it?'

'And I suppose you think it's none of mine, either.'

'I didn't say that. I just think that family matters should be discussed between the two of you, not with an outsider.'

He continued as if he hadn't heard. 'Apart from my mother, I'm Uncle Jason's only living relative and I expect that when he goes I'll come in for most of what he has to leave. Don't think I'm being crass, but being a financial advisor I'd be stupid if I didn't want to maximise his assets by encouraging him to invest wisely.'

'I see,' murmured Fiona, and she certainly did see. He didn't want to help his elderly uncle at all! He was simply interested in feathering his own nest. She wished she could find a way to warn Mr Greaves, but perhaps it wasn't necessary. He was an intelligent old chap and could probably read Aaron like a book.

'This has been lovely,' she said untruthfully, standing up to leave, 'but I must be getting home before Mother starts to worry.' Madge would do nothing of the sort but Fiona suddenly wanted to put as much distance as possible between herself and the smarmy Mr Parker.

'So what did your mother think of my friend, Jason?' Myrtle wanted to know. She had a twinkle in her eye and Fiona had the distinct impression that the urge to take part in the chase was far from dead in the older woman's heart.

'She said she thought you two were made for each other.' Fiona grinned.

'Oh, I don't know about that, but I do think we should see a bit more of each other, if only for old time's sake. How would you like to get him over here for a joint chat session, harking back to our school days? All in the cause of the book, of course!' She laughed softly. 'We could pretend that my memory is failing a bit and that I need prompting.'

'This is the twenty-first century, Myrtle. If you want to see the man, just invite him over for a meal or something.

No need to manufacture excuses.'

'Ah, but didn't you hear what he was saying? He gets nervous when women ask him over for meals. I have no intention of being seen as just one in a queue, my dear. You must have heard the old saying, softlee, softlee, catchee monkey? No, you set this up for us and he'll never suspect a thing.'

Fiona agreed to co-operate, on the grounds that some co-operation might indeed dredge up some interesting memories. On the other hand, she hoped that Myrtle wouldn't read too much into the situation.

Jason was wary of any involvement with designing women and if he rejected any advances that Myrtle might choose to make, it could all end in tears.

Her feelings must have shown on her face, because Myrtle gave a wry smile and told her not to worry.

'I know what you're thinking, dear! You're as bad as my daughter. She thinks that older people need protecting, and as I've told her more than once, I was making my own decisions and managed very well, long before she was born! As for my son, well, he thinks that anybody over forty can't possibly want to have anything to do with love. I don't argue with him, of course; what's the point? He'll find out for himself, if he lives long enough.

'I don't know if it's possible for Jason and me to rekindle the flames of our little romance but if anything comes of this I'm not going to turn my back on the possibility of a bit of future happiness just because I'm a pensioner.'

'I see,' Fiona said weakly. 'I just don't want you to get hurt, that's all. I mean, I'd feel responsible.'

'Just because you brought us together again? Jason and I live in the same town, my dear. It was only a matter of time before we came across each other. As for dealing with men,' she laughed, 'I bet I could teach you a thing or two! I've met some peculiar types in my day.'

She looked at Fiona with her head on one side. 'I suppose you haven't forgiven that young man of yours yet? Let me give you a word of advice, dear. If you really love him, don't let stubborn pride stand between you. Relationships are largely a matter of compromises, you know.'

Fiona bridled. 'What about trust and mutual respect, then? Don't they count? Jeremy let me down badly by stealing my job from me.'

'Did he really? Surely it had more to do with those Filey people who took over the newspaper. They probably didn't even know you existed, other than that you were one of a number of faceless employees at The Chronicle.

'As for your editor, he sounds a bit spineless, I admit, but possibly he feared for his own job and had to go along with the wishes of the new people at the top.'

Fiona pulled a face. 'From what he told me I gathered that he was only told to let one reporter go. The choice of which one was left up to him entirely, and he chose me, largely because

Jeremy sweet-talked his way into being kept on!'

'And you know why that was. I can understand how shocked and hurt you must have been, but it's not the end of the world. Can't you give the lad another chance?'

Fiona was very annoyed, but she tried not to let it show. Myrtle was only trying to be helpful, of course, but Madge's more sympathetic approach was what was needed now, not cold reason.

Jeremy didn't deserve a second chance and, as Mum had said, it was a jolly good thing he'd shown his true colours before he and Fiona became too deeply involved. So there!

5

Fiona decided that it was time she did some research in the newspaper files. She had reached a point where Mr Greaves seemed to have dried up as far as providing her with interesting memories went, and for her part she was at a loss to think up suitable questions.

She hoped that finding newspaper reports of his post-war triumphs would give her something to expand on.

'Speaking of the war,' Madge said, 'don't you think you should read those issues as well? You might find his name mentioned in reports mentioning local people who went overseas to fight, or lists of those who came back safely. Or what about 'evacuees arrive in Marston'. That sort of thing, I mean, you want a bit more than a bald account of who did what. You need to provide an appropriate setting for your subjects.'

Fiona groaned. 'I'd have to cover an awful lot of ground, Mum.'

'None of it will go to waste,' Madge said firmly. 'You hope to find more customers, don't you? I expect that most will be in a similar age group to Jason and Myrtle, so similar material will be needed again and again. Why, you may even end up writing a book in due course, a sort of social history of wartime Marston.'

Fiona threw up her hands, laughing. 'Steady on, Mum! One thing at a time, please. Still, you've given me some good ideas. I have an appointment at the library this morning, so I'll get started right away.'

* * *

The local library had only two micro-film readers, so it was necessary to reserve them ahead of time. Annoy-ingly, it was only possible to have them from an hour at a stretch, unless the next time slot was free when the

60

current user had finished, so Fiona had decided to book in during the day when there might be fewer researchers around.

She arrived at the library, happily looking forward to her task, but was taken aback to find Jeremy Dean already seated at the second machine.

'What are you doing here?' she demanded crossly, suddenly feeling crowded out.

'And good morning to you, too!' he responded. Fiona ignored the sarcasm.

'If I'd known you were going to be here I wouldn't have come!'

'Well, I am here, so what do you intend to do about it?'

Fiona considered stamping out, but changed her mind when she saw his mocking grin. She had as much right to be here as he did; why should she be driven out?

'I'm just going to pretend I haven't seen you!' she told him, through clenched teeth. The librarian frowned and put a finger to her lips. Embarrassed, Fiona switched on the machine and loaded in the microfilm she had chosen.

She knew what Jeremy was up to, of course. Having taken over her job he had inherited her weekly task of finding material for the popular column known as *From The Old Fyles*. Items taken from the same week, fifty, seventy-five and one hundred years ago were reproduced for the delight of today's readers.

Unfortunately this meant that he'd be coming to the library on a regular basis where she could hardly avoid meeting him. Why on earth The Chronicle didn't keep their own files in the newspaper office she couldn't think, but as they didn't possess a microfilm reader she supposed it wouldn't have been much use.

She didn't get much done that morning, unable to concentrate properly with Jeremy sitting almost within touching distance. She decided to go home for an early lunch and after that she'd go for a brisk walk to clear her head.

'That's it for today,' Jeremy said, standing up and stuffing his papers into his worn brief case. 'Back to the tread mill, I suppose.'

To her annoyance he kept pace with her as she stalked out of the building.

'Look here, Fiona,' he began, when they were standing on the stone steps leading to the street, but he was interrupted by a loud cry as she was hailed by Aaron Parker, who came bounding over to meet them.

'Miss Flint! I'm glad I've caught you. I've been meaning to speak to you again about Uncle. Look, are you free for lunch? We could discuss it over a sandwich or something.'

Jeremy's eyes were bright with interest. Much as she disliked the nerdy Aaron his arrival had come at just the right moment. Jeremy would see that she wasn't wasting her time obsessing over him, but had moved on to other things.

'I'd love to,' she murmured, and followed Aaron into the street without a backward glance. She soon regretted the impulse, however.

'Have you had a chance to sift through Uncle's papers at all?' he wondered.

'I haven't sifted through anything, as you put it, apart from looking through his old photos. As I explained before, what I'm doing doesn't involve anything like that. We just sit and talk about the good old days; he reminisces and I take notes, that's all.'

'It's highly unsatisfactory,' he sniffed. Fiona deliberately chose to misunderstand him. 'Oh, I'm sure it will all come together quite well in the end. I'm looking at the old newspapers to see if I can find mention of his awards and so on. I might even print out some of the shorter pieces and reproduce them in the booklet. Seeing them in the original type face would add to reader interest, don't you think?'

Aaron stared at her over the top of his glasses. 'Come now, Miss Flint, you surely know what I'm getting at. If I'm to help Uncle, I must get a look at his investment portfolio. Perhaps you can make an effort to see what you can find. I'd make it worth your while.'

Fiona resisted the impulse to tip her bowl of soup into his lap and run off, screaming. She was beginning to suspect there was something sinister about Aaron Parker's motives and she wanted to find out what he was up to.

During her short acquaintance with Jason Greaves she had become quite fond of the old boy and she would hate to see him taken advantage of. She put a false smile on her face and asked Aaron what he wanted her to do.

'Nothing illegal, I assure you. I just need a list of his assets, or details of his bank accounts and so on. You see, other than his pensions, Uncle doesn't have a lot to depend on. Properly re-invested that bit of money could make him much better off so he could be comfortable in his declining years, and as we all know, some are better than others. In that field, as in everything else, you get what you pay for.'

'I still don't understand why you don't ask Mr Greaves about this to his face,' she probed, hoping to get a better idea of what he was planning.

'Because he's as stubborn as they come, that's why. People of his generation mistrust things like stocks and shares because they don't understand them. As I've so often told him, he might as well keep his cash in an old sock under the mattress with an attitude like that.'

'I don't know how I'm going to manage to find what you need, but I'll try,' she lied. Really, he must think she was a gullible little fool. Jason Greaves was an astute man with all his wits about him. Very likely he, too, suspected his great-nephew's motives and that was why he avoided all talk of letting Aaron in on his financial affairs.

Aaron nodded pleasantly now he thought Fiona was on his side. As she sipped her minestrone she tried desperately to think of something she could do to foil his plans, but Mr Greaves would surely tell her off for interfering if she spoke to him.

Although many of us have relatives we don't like very much, we still don't like it when they are criticised by outsiders. Should she go to the police? That wouldn't do, either. She had to get proof before she could go to them, and that meant stringing Aaron along.

'How is your soup?' she asked sweetly. 'Mine is delicious.'

'Very nice,' he answered.

★　★　★

Myrtle put on a very nice meal for Jason and the Flints. They all enjoyed it, for quite different reasons.

'It's lovely to have a home-cooked meal that one hasn't prepared oneself,' Madge remarked. 'I mean, I do go out to restaurants occasionally, but it's not the same, is it?'

'But I take my turn with the cooking,' Fiona protested.

'I know you do, dear, and very nice it is, too, but here we have the best of both worlds, you see? Enjoying someone else's food in different surroundings.'

She was doing her best to keep up a flow of conversation, trying to break the ice between Myrtle and her elderly swain, but as things turned out Jason was quite relaxed for once.

'I do like a good old-fashioned steak and kidney pud,' he beamed. 'Something a man can get his teeth into. Much better than all that quiche and salad stuff they want to ram down a fellow's throat nowadays.'

'I'm so glad you're enjoying it.' Myrtle smiled. 'And there's plums and custard to follow. I did think of making my special treacle tart, but I thought it might be too heavy on top of the suet pudding.'

'Maybe next time,' he told her.

Fiona and Madge exchanged a conspiratorial glance. 'The way to a man's heart,' Madge mouthed, surreptitiously unbuttoning the waistband of her corduroy skirt.

She must remember to do it up again later, she reminded herself, or she might disgrace herself when she stood up. Not that Jason would notice; he was too busy shovelling down their friend's good cooking.

'More cauliflower?' Myrtle asked, moving a covered dish in his direction. Fiona noticed that his wrinkled face was wreathed in smiles as he nodded agreement. Was this cupboard love, she wondered, or was he beginning to show a more than friendly interest in his childhood sweetheart?

'That went well, didn't it?' Madge remarked, when he and her daughter were on their way home. 'Do you think there's anything in it? Shall we be turning up at St Mark's in due course, looking glamorous in flowery dresses and big hats?'

'You were the one who warned me against match-making,' Fiona reminded her. 'Actually, Mum, I wish it would come to something. They'd be good for each other, I think.'

'Love can strike at any age,' Madge said dreamily. 'It isn't only for the young.'

'That's not what I meant, exactly. Listen, I want to run something by you, Mum, something that has to do with Mr Greaves.'

'This sounds serious.'

'I think it may be. You've heard him speak of his great-nephew, Aaron Parker?'

'Yes, and I gather there's no love lost between them.'

'Exactly. Well, I've bumped into Aaron a couple of times now, although whether we've met by accident or design I don't know. The thing is, Mum, he's trying to find out about the state of Mr Greaves' finances on the pretext of helping him with his investments, and he's asked me to see what I can find out.'

'Cheek!'

'I suspect he's up to no good, so I pretended to go along with it, to find out what he wants to know. I shan't really try to snoop of course, but I'll just let him think that's what I'm doing.'

Madge's jaw dropped. 'Oh, no, you don't, my girl. You stay well out of it. For one thing you don't want to be involved if things fall apart and the police start an investigation into Aaron's doings.

'For another, your relationship with your customers has to be completely above board if this ghost writing scheme of yours is going to work. Nobody will want to deal with you if it gets out that you're prying into things which don't concern you.'

'Well, as I said, I'm not really going to start going through drawers, or asking awkward questions. I'm only pretending to go along with what Aaron has in mind, hoping that he'll give himself away.'

'Even so, I don't like it.'

Fiona remained noncommittal, but she had no intention of giving up so easily. As it happened she had no chance to do anything because a few days later Mr Greaves came down with a heavy cold and told her not to call round.

'I be a great believer in keeping germs to byself,' he croaked. 'I be going to bed now with a hot toddy. I'll let you know when it's safe to cub back.'

'That's quite all right, Mr Greaves. I want to spend more time in the library in any case. By the time you're feeling better I should have some interesting things to show you.' She hung up the phone after wishing him a speedy recovery.

She spent the next few days treasure hunting in The Chronicle's old files. One of the library's microfilm readers had the capacity of making photocopies of items which had been printed in the documents or old newspapers.

Because it was necessary to put a coin in the slot for each print-out Fiona wanted to keep this activity to a minimum or the cost would soon mount up, but it certainly saved a lot of time when she needed a complete article. Like many modern reporters who worked from a mini tape recorder she had never learned shorthand.

Scrolling through the pages of issues taken around the time that Myrtle came to Marston as a child she was delighted to find a photo that some enterprising photographer had taken of a group of evacuees at the railway station. Herded together on the platform, the children had gas masks slung over their shoulders and most were clutching small suitcases or bulging pillow cases.

According to the information written below, the youngsters had just arrived and were waiting for their prospective hosts to come to claim them. Remembering what Myrtle had told her, Fiona felt a pang of sympathy for those long-ago children who had been sent away from home, not knowing if they would ever see their parents again.

How awful it must have been to

stand shivering in your shoes, hoping to be chosen by a nice family, and, if you were rather plain, seeing the pretty ones chosen first.

Fiona had a sudden recollection of being left until last when the children in her elementary school class were picking up sides for games and having to suffer the humiliation of being added to one of the teams by a kindly teacher.

She stared at the photo, trying to work out if one of the older girls could have been Myrtle. The one with the long plaits might have been her, but it was hard to tell from a small black and white image.

Carefully centering the picture on the screen she popped a coin into the slot and waited for the sheet to appear. She would call at Myrtle's on her way home and see if she recognised anyone.

'Here you are at last! I was beginning to think you'd forgotten all about me,' Myrtle blurted, when she came to the door in response to Fiona's ring. Her eyes widened when she saw who her visitor was.

'Who were expecting?' Fiona said cheerfully. 'Someone to tell you you've won the lottery?'

'Come inside, dear. No, I've been waiting for Jason. He was supposed to come here for lunch today, but he's half an hour late and there's been no word from him. No word at all, and it's not like him to be discourteous. I don't think he's been eating properly because of his cold, so I invited him here to feed him up.'

At any other time Fiona might have made a joke about this, but Myrtle was clearly worried so she simply suggested that Mr Greaves might have mistaken the time or even the day. Myrtle shook her head.

'I don't see how he could. I rang him first thing this morning with my invitation, and told him to come at noon. Now it's almost one and he still isn't here.'

'Have you telephoned?'

'Of course I have, dear, and there's no answer.'

'Then he must have left the house by now. Maybe the bus broke down or something and he had to wait for another one to come along.'

'No, something is wrong, Fiona. Very wrong. I can sense it. I'd like you to go over there and see if there's any sign of him. Would you do that for me?'

'Certainly, if it would make you feel any happier.'

So Fiona set off on foot, taking a number of short cuts which soon brought her to Mr Greaves' home. She knew that the older man, perhaps still weak from his illness, would have found such a long walk too much for him and so he would have travelled the round-about route by bus.

Although she rapped at the door and called his name several times, there was no sign of Mr Greaves. He must have left earlier as planned, and might even now be safely seated at Myrtle's table, tucking into the meal she'd provided.

She didn't want to leave without finding some clue to his whereabouts, so on impulse she went round to the back door and knocked there. Still no answer.

The curtains in what she knew to be his sitting-room weren't quite closed, and when she peered in with her nose to the glass she was appalled to see his crumpled figure stretched out on the carpet. Pulling her cell phone out of her bag she hastily dialled 999, asking for an ambulance to be sent at once.'

'And we'd better have the police, too,' she added. 'The house is all locked up and they may have to break in.'

Then she leaned against the wall and waited for help to arrive, hoping against hope that Mr Greaves hadn't suffered a fatal heart attack.

6

Fiona waited anxiously while the investigating constable forced his way into the house, closely followed by two ambulance attendants carrying a stretcher. A little crowd of neighbours had quickly gathered, all wanting to know what had happened.

'I've seen you round here before,' one woman said, looking Fiona up and down suspiciously. 'You're not a relative, are you?'

'Mr Greaves is writing his memoirs, and I'm helping him,' she answered, feeling that this wasn't the time or place for a more detailed explanation. 'He was supposed to have lunch with friends today and when he didn't turn up, they were worried and asked me to make sure he was all right.' Again, she was careful to avoid mentioning the fact that Myrtle was a female friend or that would start rumours flying.

'And he must be far from all right if you had to send for an ambulance and the cops,' the woman said. 'P'haps he's dead. Murdered, even.'

Her eyes were bright with excitement and Fiona felt that she couldn't know the poor man very well or she would have shown proper concern rather than this ghoulish interest.

At that moment the attendants emerged from the house carrying their patient on the stretcher. As they carefully loaded him into the waiting ambulance, Fiona was glad to see that he had been fitted with an oxygen mask which meant he was still alive.

A dressing on his forehead had already turned an ominous pink colour, but as far as she could tell, there were no other signs of injury. No slings or splints were in evidence, but who knew what might be going on internally? It would take a doctor to decide that.

'Which of you found the victim and

made the call to the emergency services?'

The constable had come out of the house and was now addressing the group. Fiona indicated that she was the one he needed to talk to, and at his request she followed him into the house.

'What happened to Mr Greaves?' she wanted to know. 'Could the ambulance people tell you anything? Was it a heart attack, or a fall?'

'Sorry, Miss. I'll ask the questions, if you don't mind. I'd like you to sit down, please. I don't want you to disturb anything at the crime scene.'

Crime scene! Fiona's mouth opened and shut wordlessly. She'd more or less been told to mind her own business and she'd probably learn more if she sat still and followed the drift of his questions.

'I'd like you to tell me how you came to find the victim, Mr Greaves.'

'Well, when he didn't answer the door, I assumed he must be at home, so I went round to the back. That door was locked as well so I looked through the window and saw him lying on the floor, and that's when I called for help.'

'How did you know he needed help, Miss?'

For some reason this annoyed Fiona and she said tartly, 'Why else would he have been lying on the floor in an awkward position if he wasn't in difficulty? Studying the pattern on the carpet or something? As far as I know he hasn't taken up yoga so I naturally assumed that something had happened, an attack of some kind, or a fall.'

The constable gave her an old-fashioned look. 'Never mind all that. What were you doing here in the first place?' Patiently she explained about her working relationship with Jason and Myrtle; how Jason had a lunch date with Myrtle but had failed to turn up at the appointed time.

'We thought that he must have been delayed or even become confused about the time. I thought there must be some rational explanation like that, and told

Mrs Siddons as much.

'I think she agreed up to the point where she didn't want to bother the police — that would have annoyed him very much if all this had turned out to be a storm in a teacup — yet she was worried enough to ask me to come over here to check on him, which of course I did.'

'And are you quite sure that both the front and back doors were securely locked?'

'Yes, they were. Not that I'm in the habit of walking to Mr Greaves' home without permission, but I certainly would have in the case of an emergency.'

'What about next of kin? They'll have to be notified.'

'As far as I know he doesn't have too many relatives,' Fiona told him. 'He's a widower, and he and his wife never had any children. There is a sister somewhere, and a great nephew, but neither of them live locally and I'm afraid I don't know their addresses, or where they can be reached.'

The constable nodded. 'Before you go, I'd like you to look around and tell me if you think anything has gone missing.'

'I'll try, but you must realise that there are rooms in this house I've never been into. I've never been upstairs, for example, and even here, I've no idea what might have been in the various drawers and cupboards other than those where he kept his photograph albums.'

Her gaze went to the photo of Mr Greaves' late wife. 'As far as I know, that picture frame is real silver. He treasures that photo. I'd have thought that a burglar would have taken that. It's the sort of thing that could be easily sold and never traced.'

The constable took her up on that immediately. 'What makes you think there was a burglar, Miss? I said nothing about that, did I? Perhaps you know more about this than you're letting on!'

'Oh, for goodness' sake! I came here and found my friend in a crumpled heap on the floor, with what now looks like a head injury, and you said something about not disturbing the scene of the crime! I can put two and two together as well as the next person. Mr Greaves wouldn't have hit himself over the head, would he? I expect this was a burglary gone wrong.'

'That remains to be seen, Miss. Now, I have your name and address in my notebook, so you may as well get off now.'

Used to watching television mysteries, Fiona half expected him to tell her not to leave the country without permission, but he said nothing more. With a heavy heart she set out to let Myrtle know that her delicious lunch would not be needed now.

*   *   *

When she heard the news, Myrtle put a hand to her mouth to stifle a cry of horror which threatened to turn into full-blown hysteria. Fortunately the old wartime survival spirit came to the fore and with a great effort she was able to pull herself together.

'Poor old chap! What a nasty thing to happen. Is he going to be all right?'

'They wouldn't tell me a thing,' Fiona replied. 'I suppose they really didn't know anything until he was seen by a doctor.'

'Right, then. We'll phone the hospital and find out. I imagine he's in the Marston General?'

Fiona nodded. She didn't want to say that he'd probably be transferred to a trauma unit in the city if things were as bad as they'd looked to her.

'Well, what are we waiting for? Call them and find out.'

'Are you a relative?' the disembodied voice asked when she got through to the hospital.

'No, just a friend, but . . . '

'I'm sorry. We can only give that information out to the next of kin.'

Fiona hung up in disgust.

'What did they say, Fiona? Is he going to recover?'

'They wouldn't tell me anything because I'm not a relative,' Fiona said miserably.

Myrtle looked at her in exasperation. 'Oh, really! We'll see about that! Just give me that phone!'

From the way the conversation went, Fiona assumed that her friend was being given the same runaround that she herself had just experienced.

Thus she was shocked to hear Myrtle say, 'No, he doesn't have any next of kin, as such, but I'm his fiancée and I insist on seeing him.'

The response was obviously satisfactory because as she replaced the receiver she turned to Fiona and said, 'We can see him this evening. The Ward Sister couldn't tell me anything except that Jason has regained consciousness, but apparently she'll ask the doctor in charge to fill me in.

'Myrtle! How lovely. You and Jason

are engaged? I had no idea,' Fiona beamed.

Myrtle blushed. 'Neither does Jason, actually, but I'm working on it.'

'Then let's hope he doesn't have a fit when the Sister tells him that his fiancée is on her way to see him.'

'I'll tell him that the bump on the head has made him lose his memory and forget that he proposed to me,' Myrtle quipped. 'You'll come with me to the hospital, of course?'

'Wild horses couldn't keep me away,' Fiona said. 'I must dash home now, but I'll be back in plenty of time to get you there before visiting hours start.'

*　*　*

As she walked through the damp streets her mind was working furiously. It was possible that Mr Greaves had surprised a burglar and been struck down when he resisted, but what if it hadn't been a real burglar at all?

What if it had been Aaron Parker,

searching for those all-important documents and interrupted by his great uncle?

Or what if the two had had an argument concerning Aaron wanting to take charge of Mr Greaves' financial affairs? She could imagine the older man giving an indignant refusal, Aaron losing his temper and striking out and then fleeing the scene when he realised what he's done, perhaps leaving his victim for dead . . .

A lot would hinge on what Mr Greaves had to say now that he had regained consciousness. Fiona couldn't wait to hear what that might be.

* * *

Fiona and Myrtle found it infuriating when they were made to wait outside the ward when they arrived at the hospital. Visitors were arriving from all directions, carrying flowers and magazines and bags of fruit, but a nurse headed them off when they paused just inside the door, searching for Mr Greaves.

'What's happened to him? Has he been moved, or what?' Myrtle demanded, looking very much her age now that her customary cheerful expression had been wiped off her face.

'We've put the screens around his bed because he's being interviewed by the police,' they were told. 'You can go in as soon as they've finished.'

'They would come during visiting hours, of course!' Myrtle complained. 'Cutting back the time we have to spend with him. Surely they could have left all that until later?'

'I expect they need to find out the details as soon as they can if they're to have any chance of catching those responsible,' Fiona murmured. 'The longer they leave it the harder it will be.'

'They won't catch the man,' Myrtle said. 'How could they? He won't have left any fingerprints. Burglars know enough to wear gloves nowadays, don't they? And if you're right and nothing was stolen, that's another clue down the drain.

'Let's say his bits and pieces turned up on a market stall somewhere, the police might trace them back to the person selling them, but as it is they won't have any leads. And what I'm afraid of is that if Jason frightened him off, the man will turn up again at a later date and this time the poor dear might not escape so easily.'

'I doubt that would happen,' Fiona soothed, but her mind was still working furiously. What if it had been Aaron? Should she mention her suspicions to the police?

At that moment the police officer emerged from behind the screens, pulling back the curtains as he came. It was the same man who had interviewed Fiona at the scene of the crime. As he strode out of the ward he gave her a cursory glance, but didn't speak.

'I suppose we can go in now,' Myrtle said, not waiting to find out. She teetered into the ward on her high heels with Fiona trotting behind.

Mr Greaves was lying back on a pile of pillows, looking wan. He was dressed in a pair of washed-out striped pyjamas, which were probably hospital issue because he hadn't been in a position to bring anything with him when he was carried out of his house by the ambulance attendants.

'How are you feeling, dear?' Myrtle asked, looking deeply concerned.

'I've felt better,' he grumbled. 'It's coming to something when you can't go into your own home without being attacked. Criminals get off too lightly nowadays, that's the problem. Makes 'em think they can do what they like without fear of punishment. They should bring back the cat, that's what I say.'

Fiona looked confused. Cat? What cat? Was his mind wandering? Myrtle guessed what she was thinking and said 'the cat o' nine tails. Something they used to beat convicts with in the olden days.'

Fiona ignored the history lesson. 'Do you know what happened, Mr Greaves?'

He raised his eyes to the ceiling. 'That's what the copper asked me. Of course, I know! Not in my dotage yet, am I?'

'Well?' Myrtle prompted.

'Oh, all right! I'd been along to the chemist's to renew my arthritis prescription and I went home to change before coming to have lunch with you.

'I let myself into the house and I got the shock of my life when I saw this big bruiser, going through my desk. Well, if I'd been a few years younger I might have tackled him, but as things are I thought I'd better make a hasty retreat.

'Trouble was, I can't move too quickly and I suppose he caught up to me and did me a mischief. That's all I remember, but to judge by this lump on my head he must have walloped me with something.' He felt his scalp gingerly.

'Were you able to give the police a description of the man?' Fiona wondered. If it was Aaron he would have known him at once, of course.

Mr Greaves shook his head, wincing as he did so.

'Tall, burly, fairly young, I'd say, by the way he held himself. He was wearing a boiler suit like mechanics wear, and he had one of those stocking things over his face. Made him look like a hallowe'en ghoul.'

Myrtle made soothing noises. 'Never mind, it's all over now. You stay in here for a bit and have a good rest and you'll be back to your self in no time.'

'How did the man get in?' Fiona wondered. She was sure she hadn't seen any sign of forced entry at the house. Both front and back doors had been intact, and there were no broken windows.

'He must have let himself in with my spare key,' Mr Greaves said crossly. 'I keep one under the flower pot near the door in case I ever lock myself out when I step outside to bring in the milk or the newspaper. That copper gave me a right telling off, too. Told me it was an open invitation to thieves to leave a key there. Nonsense, I said. We all do it, don't we?'

That was the trouble; everyone did do it. Fiona made a mental note to move their own key away from its hiding place under the birdbath. It was probably the first place that a would-be burglar would look, although she suspected that younger villains wouldn't bother. They'd just smash a window and gain access that way.

'So you didn't recognise the thief at all?' she persisted. 'You didn't know his voice, for instance?'

'He didn't say a word, did he? Not that it would have helped if he had. I don't mix with that class of person as a rule.'

'You'll have to get the locks changed now,' Myrtle was saying. 'Would you like me to handle that for you?' The unspoken message was that the burglar had probably taken the spare key with him, and might come back to finish the job.

'I suppose so,' Mr Greaves said wearily. 'Nothing much I can do about it, is there, stuck in here. You do what you can, Myrtle, and you won't find me ungrateful.'

She left then, with promises to return the next day. 'I could kill that rotten burglar, I could really!' she snapped, when she and Fiona were walking away from the hospital. 'It's all very well to patch him up and send him back home, but even with new locks on the doors, will he ever feel safe there again? That's the pity of it all.'

Fiona agreed, but her own thoughts went off on another direction, one which she wasn't prepared to discuss with her friend. As far as she was concerned, all the evidence pointed towards Aaron Parker.

Why wear a boiler suit, if not to conceal clothing which his great uncle might recognise? Then, too, the baggy garment would disguise his figure to some extent.

An ordinary thief would probably have worn the jeans, sweatshirt and trainers which was the common uniform among the young, undistinguishable in a crowd.

Mr Greaves had caught the man riffling through his desk: didn't that point to Aaron, too? Why not collect such small valuables, with some resale value, as were lying around, before making a hasty exit? She knew she was clutching at straws.

The fellow could have been looking for money, or credit cards, which a householder might logically keep in a desk drawer. Once again, she wished she could think of some way of forcing Aaron into the open.

7

Fiona had come to the conclusion that she should discuss the problem with Jeremy. She still didn't mean to let him back into her life, but this was different.

Being a trained newspaper reporter like herself, his thought processes ran along parallel lines and also he knew where to go to uncover various facts. In a way, reporters solved mysteries every day, getting to the bottom of breaking stories and flushing out the facts.

She found Jeremy in the library, still seeking out ancient items of interest for the bygones column. He looked up, pleased, when she approached him.

'Can you leave that for a bit? I need to speak to you.'

'Sure! Fire ahead.'

'Not here,' she told him, turning away from the librarian's hawk-like gaze. 'Let's go for a walk. It's not raining much, just a bit of drizzle.'

He got up at once, reaching for his raincoat. 'Where do you want to go?'

'Down along the canal bank, I think.'

Apart from a man walking his dog there was nobody else about at this time of day. The rain distorted the waters of the canal and even the ducks seemed to have disappeared for once.

Jeremy fell into step beside Fiona and she was very much aware of his presence at her side. The old chemistry hadn't gone away, but this was not the time to dwell on that.

'So, what's this all about?' he asked, when they had been walking for several minutes. 'I'm happy to see you, of course, but I mustn't stay out here long. I'm supposed to be working.'

'Do you remember that man who met me when we were leaving the library the other day?'

'That chap who took you off to lunch? Sure, what about him?'

'His name is Aaron Parker. His great uncle, Jason Greaves, is a client of mine, a very nice old boy.'

'Isn't he the man who was attacked in his home yesterday? I have a story ready for this week's Chronicle. Crime in Marston, and all that. Villains preying on elderly war veteran. He fought for his country, only to come to this. Sob stuff. Should sell papers.'

Fiona regarded him with distaste. 'Mr Greaves may be only a statistic to you, but he's a human being to me, a very nice person who doesn't deserve to make the headlines in this manner.'

'Whoa!' Jeremy raised both hands in a mock display of fending off an attack. 'No need to get worked up! I agree with you wholeheartedly, but I do have a job to do; you know that. So where does this Parker person come in?'

'I think it's highly possible that he was the intruder, Jeremy.'

'Then why not go to the police?'

'Because I don't have any proof, that's why. Besides, there's something else. If the police question him and they let slip that I'm the one who turned him in, he's likely to drop me in it as well.'

'What? How could he?'

She sighed. 'Mum warned me about this. Well, Aaron is some kind of financial advisor, and he wants to take over Mr Greaves' affairs as a favour to him. To maximise his profits, he says, whatever that means. The trouble is, uncle isn't interested.'

'So our Aaron wants you to use your womanly wiles to persuade the old boy, is that it?'

'It's a bit more than that, I'm afraid. He asked me to try to get details of Mr Greaves' investments, bank account numbers and so on.'

'To which you said no, of course.'

Fiona blushed. 'Actually, I agreed to do as he asked.'

'You what!' Jeremy stared at her as if he couldn't believe what she'd just said.

'Oh, I had no intention of actually doing anything,' she admitted. 'I just pretended to go along with it, thinking I could keep an eye on him that way. He might let his guard down and I'd be able to get proof of what he was up to, and be able to protect Mr Greaves, you see?'

'I see, all right, and now you've got yourself into a right mess. You wonder if Aaron was the masked intruder, but you can't tell the police about his plans or you'd be pegged as an accomplice.

'Oh, the big dailies will have a field day when you come up in court, Fiona Flint! Petty crook, trying to bilk pensioners out of their savings, gaining access to their homes by pretending to record their life stories. They could really get their teeth into this one.'

'I know.' She looked so miserable that he was on the verge of taking her into his arms, until he thought better of it.

'So where do I come in?'

'I don't know, really. I thought perhaps you could dig into Aaron's background and see if there's anything which doesn't add up.

'Has he been involved in any scams, for instance.'

'Why can't you do it? You're just as capable as I am of getting to the bottom of a story.'

'I can't, can I? He'd be sure to suspect something. You, on the other hand, could talk to him, or visit his place of work, as a bona fide reporter on some story or other.'

'I suppose I could have a go,' he said doubtfully.

He had only a fleeting sympathy for Mr Greaves, for after all he didn't even know the man, but he hated to see Fiona looking so downcast.

When she had stormed out of the office that day he had decided to cut his losses; when it came to pretty girls there were plenty more fish in the sea.

It had come as a shock to him to realise how deeply he felt about her, and he would have given a lot to have put things right between them. Maybe this was his chance.

'So tell me everything you know about this Parker man.'

'That's just it, I don't know very

much at all. His grandfather was Mr Greaves' brother. He's dead now, but he has a daughter, Rita, living in Southampton I think. Aaron is her son.'

'Surely he doesn't live in Southampton as well, if he keeps popping up here? It's miles away.'

'I know, but he doesn't seem to live here in Marston, either. He's not in the phone book, or the business directory.'

'His place of work, then. Does he have his own company, or is he employed by some larger organisation?'

Fiona shrugged helplessly. 'That's the problem. You know how many businesses have fancy names. It could be anything.'

Jeremy scratched his nose. 'I hate to say this, but I don't think we're going to get anywhere without some sort of starting point to go on.'

Fiona's heart leapt. He had said we! She brightened up immediately.

'I'll just have to pump him for information, then, won't I?'

'Forget it! The farther you stay away

from that guy, the better. If it is Aaron that bopped your Mr Greaves over the head it means he doesn't hesitate when it comes to violence.

'You could be in danger, never mind getting on the wrong side of the police. If you've any sense you'll go to them and come clean before you get in any deeper. Tell them how you led him on and perhaps they'll believe that you weren't in on the scam, if scam it is.'

'What are you going to do with nothing to go on? If they start asking him questions it'll put him on his guard. What we need is proof, Jeremy, and the only way to get it is for me to talk to him again, and hope he trips himself up.'

He sighed. 'I suppose you're right, but how do you propose to get in touch with him if you don't know where he lives or works?'

'If my theory is right, and he didn't find what he was looking for at Mr Greaves' house, then he'll be in touch with me. Plan B, if you like.'

'I still don't like it, but I suppose it's the only way. Just be careful, though, all right? No going down dark alleys when he's around, and all that.'

Fiona promised to keep her wits about her. Not that she needed the warning. She hadn't taken to Aaron from that first day when he'd barged into his uncle's house, and now that she suspected him of robbery with violence she had no illusions as to what could happen to her if she was careless.

★   ★   ★

It was some time before Aaron came back into the picture. Just when she was beginning to think she had imagined his involvement in the assault on Mr Greaves he turned up again at the library.

She jumped when a hand descended on her shoulder and twisted around to find him smiling down at her.

'I thought I might find you here,' he said. 'Are you free for lunch? I wanted to talk to you about our little arrangement.'

'Yes, I can leave this for now,' she replied, her heart thumping painfully.

He looked so ordinary and so pleasant that she immediately had her doubts about him. After all, Mr Greaves was his own flesh and blood.

Fiona did her best to create an impression of a not too bright young woman who was over-awed by the handsome young businessman sitting across the table from her.

Not that she did find him attractive, he wasn't her type, but if she wanted to find out what she needed to know, a facade of breathless admiration seemed the right way to go.

'Does your boss mind you taking long lunch hours like this?' she asked, with a low cunning.

'Oh, I'm self employed,' he laughed, 'so the boss doesn't mind at all.'

'Really! I believe you're something in the world of banking. Isn't that what you told me the last time we met?'

This was a technique that Fiona often used when interviewing a subject. She had learned that people just love to prove somebody else wrong, and would pontificate at length to set her straight.

It was just as effective now. Aaron treated her to a long discourse, filled with jargon. The upshot was that he took people's money and invested it for them, receiving a commission for himself.

'And of course the more profit they make, the better I do out of it.'

'How wonderful. You must be very clever at it. I'm sure I could never do anything like that.'

Fiona was not in the habit of fluttering her eyelashes at a man, preferring to be her natural, up front self, but on this occasion she came close to it.

'No, I don't suppose you could,' he answered, with what was close to a sneer.

For a moment she felt annoyed and had to remind herself that she was playing a part. It was no good taking umbrage and frightening him off.

'So I expect you have your own company, then?'

'Yes, that's right.'

'So what's it called, then?'

'Money Works. It's a play on words. Rather clever, don't you think?'

'Oh. I see. You take the clients' money and put it to work for them, right?'

He took a sip of wine but didn't answer immediately, so she had to try another tack.

'I don't think I've seen your office in my travels around town. Are you fairly new to Marston, then?'

'Actually I'm in Palmerston Magna, but my clients are drawn from a wide area, so I'm quite often over here on business.'

'And of course you come over to see Uncle Jason.'

He shot her a quick look, but she was careful to keep her face impassive and he seemed satisfied that she didn't mean anything in particular by that.

'Speaking of Uncle Jason, I'm hoping you'll be able to get results for me soon.'

'Oh, I know I'm supposed to ask him about his investments,' Fiona murmured, 'but I don't like to bother him while he's still in hospital. After such a nasty bump on the head, any worry might give him a setback.'

Aaron put his hands to his lips in an attitude of prayer, although she was sure that any spiritual thoughts were far from his mind.

'Why don't we go over there and have a look around before he's released from the hospital? Then we won't need to worry him at all,' he said piously.

'Hmm,' Fiona said, stalling for time.

Not only did she have no intention of snooping around someone else's private home, but she also wondered why Aaron had suggested this. Did it mean that he wasn't the intruder after all?

Could it have been sheer bad luck that poor Mr Greaves had been targeted by a stranger at the very point in his life when his great nephew was also trying to take him for a ride?

'Do you really think we ought to do this?' she said at last, 'and how are we going to get inside? Do you have a key?'

'Never you mind, Fiona. Let's just say I have my methods. I'll phone the hospital later today and get an update on his condition. After all, we don't want him arriving home and catching us in the act, do we?'

'We certainly don't want him to do that!' Fiona replied, putting a wealth of meaning into her tone, which he either failed to pick up on, or chose to ignore. 'Just give me your phone number and I'll get in touch when I'm free to join you.'

'No, no. You give me yours and I'll phone you.'

She was half inclined not to comply, but what good would that have done?

Her mother was listed in the phone book, the only Flint in Marston, so anyone could track them down in minutes.

⋆ ⋆ ⋆

After leaving the restaurant she went straight home and phoned Jeremy at The Chronicle. He answered at once.

'What did you find out?' he demanded. 'Do you have a good bio on our friend?'

'He's being very cagey, but I do know that his company is called Money Works, and he lives at Palmerston Magna. Unfortunately it isn't listed in the business directory or the phone book, and neither is he.'

'That's odd,' Jeremy mused.

Fiona heard the crackle of paper which probably meant that Jeremy was about to consume one of his favourite chocolate bars.

His next words were somewhat muffled and she guessed that he had his teeth sunk in a slab of chocolate-coated caramel.

'If he has a small outfit he probably works from home,' he mumbled. 'I bet he has a website. That's the way to go nowadays. Funny he hasn't a phone, though, but I expect he's new in the district and hasn't got a listing in the phone book yet. There may be one online. Look, I've got to go, or I'll have old Kemp breathing down my neck. I'll be in touch.'

Still feeling jumpy, Fiona decided that it was time she took Myrtle Siddons into her confidence, so she raced over to her house and was lucky enough to find her at home.

'Hello, dear. I've just got back from visiting Jason.'

'How is he?'

'I'm a bit worried, actually. The doctor says he's coming along nicely as far as recovering from the concussion and the head wound goes. Of course, they don't know him as well as I do, and he still looks frail to me.

'People of our age can't take that sort of shock and expect to bounce back immediately, not that a person of any age would shrug off that sort of attack without a second thought.'

'There's something I have to tell you, Myrtle, but first I need your promise that you'll say nothing to anybody, particularly not to Mr Greaves.'

'Of course, dear. I'm the soul of discretion. You can rely on me.'

Myrtle waited expectantly for Fiona to begin, but as the tale unfolded she began to look more and more indignant, leaning back in her chair with her fingers drumming on the tweed-covered arms.

'So you see why I daren't go to the police,' Fiona said at last.

'I do indeed, dear. Then I tell you what I'm going to do. I'm going to spring Jason from that hospital and bring him here. I'll tell him it's to convalesce, because he needs someone to look after him, and I know he won't be keen to go home just now, after what

113

happened to him there.

'We'll let the hospital think otherwise, though, so that Aaron won't be able to track him down. Meanwhile, you see if you can get any evidence on our Mr Parker. And do be careful!'

8

'I've managed to get the goods on Aaron Parker,' Jeremy announced. Fiona had just washed her hair and had almost missed the call, which had come just as she was wrapping her head in a towel.

'Great!' she enthused, dealing with a soaking lock that threatened to send a rivulet of cold water seeping under the collar of her dressing gown. 'I hope he's wanted by the police and we can wrap up this investigation as soon as possible.'

'Well, no, I haven't quite got that far,' he admitted. 'I have found his website, though.'

Fiona bit back a sarcastic comment. Given a bit of patience, anyone could find a website by using a search engine. It was hardly rocket science.

'Are you still there, Fiona? Look, it's not much, but there's no address for his company. Prospective clients are directed to contact him by e-mail, or write to a post office box number. That smells fishy to me.'

'I don't know. Lots of people work from home these days. It saves the expense of renting office space. As for the website, it may be that he invests money for people outside Britain, such as ex-pats living in Spain or somewhere.'

'Who knows? What I'm more interested in now is why he's so anxious to get hold of his uncle's cash.'

'Because Mr Greaves' money is being under-utilised, as he puts it.' Fiona was merely playing devil's advocate now. 'One of the last things Aaron said to me was that he was concerned about his uncle's health, especially now, since the attack. The time may come when he has to go into some sort of nursing home, and having plenty of money would make the difference between a comfortable place and some sort of cut-rate establishment with minimum resources.

'And you know, Jeremy, there is something to that. It's true that I don't trust Aaron, and I certainly get the impression that he's greedy and selfish, but don't you see, that may be the real reason behind all this. Suppose Mr Greaves does need help. Who will have to find the money for extras if he doesn't have enough? His niece, probably. Aaron may be trying to look out for his mother.'

'That idea won't fly. The old boy owns his house, doesn't he? He could sell up and use the cash from that, if he has to.'

'That won't bring much, surely? It's a nice enough place but it's just a semi in a side street. Hardly Buckingham Palace.'

'That's what you think! Similar houses in that district are fetching as much as £200,000 at present.'

Fiona let out a long whistle. If that was true, she wondered how young couples, starting out, could ever afford to buy a home of their own.

'The information on his site indicates that he has a highly-successful company with scores of investors,' Jeremy went on. 'You know the sort of thing; glowing testimonials from satisfied customers.'

'That could be all hype,' Fiona said. 'I mean, he's hardly likely to say 'struggling entrepreneur desperate for customers' is he?'

'No, but I'm going to follow this up. I'll contact him through the Money Works website, pretending I have money to invest, and I'll ask to be put in touch with some of those enthusiastic clients. They're only identified as 'Mrs Brown, Cheshire' and so on. I'll ask for bank references as well. Then we'll see what he has to say. It's a reasonable thing to ask.

'Nobody would throw away good money without first establishing whether the firm is trustworthy. There are so many scams on the Internet these days and the police are always putting out warnings, telling people to look before they leap. Seniors are particularly vulnerable, as you know.'

'Sounds good to me. Good luck with that. Look, I have to go, I'm dripping all over the carpet. Let me know how things work out.'

Smartly dressed in navy trousers and a pink shirt worn underneath a dark blue fleece waistcoat, with her hair looking soft and glossy, Fiona set off to interview a new client.

This was a Mrs Barnet — 'call me Flora' — who had been referred by Myrtle, a friend from the church ladies' guild. She lived in a large house on the Palmerston Road, and was the widow of an army colonel who had recently died.

'I don't know if this is the sort of thing you do,' she boomed, when Fiona was seated in the over-furnished dining-room, being plied with tea and scones. 'I don't want my life story done, you understand. It's the life of my late husband, Alfred, I want to see in print. He had such an interesting career and travelled all over the world in the service.

'Now, about your fee,' Mrs Barnet said briskly. Fiona's heart sank. Was this another of those women who hoped to beat down the price, not understanding that printing costs made up the greater part of the amount? But that wasn't the case.

'I can pay your deposit, but I'm afraid the rest will have to wait until the book is delivered to me.'

Fiona relaxed. 'That's quite all right, Mrs Barnet. In fact, that's how I always work. I don't accept the balance of the fee until the books have been delivered to the customer and approved by him or her.'

This was a bit of a stretch, of course, as the work she was doing for Myrtle and Mr Greaves had yet to be completed, but this was how she intended to operate, feeling confident that she could do a good job which her customers would find acceptable.

'You mustn't get the idea that I'm

short of money,' Mrs Barnet remarked, with a girlish laugh. 'The colonel has left me well fixed, oh, yes indeed.'

'Of course not,' Fiona began, feeling a bit embarrassed. The women's finances were nothing to do with her and she hoped she wasn't about to be treated to a deluge of private information. However, once started, Mrs Barnet rambled on.

'I don't suppose you understand this, a girl of your age, just starting out in life, but we older people live on our investments. This means that we can't get hold of large sums of money at a moment's notice. We have to wait for our dividends to come in. You do understand about dividends?'

'Oh, yes,' Fiona murmured.

'So you know, then, that my income arrives at fixed intervals. It's from some of that money that I'll be paying you.'

This was more than Fiona wanted to know and she wondered why Mrs Barnet felt it necessary to confide in her.

Surely it wasn't wise to blurt out such details to a complete stranger? But her attention sharpened when she heard the name Money Works.

'Such a nice young man, a Mr Parker. He handles my money personally, you know, instead of handing over my account to one of his assistants. I don't even have to go to his office to sign papers.

'He always calls at the house with them, such wonderful service in this day and age, don't you think?'

'Yes, indeed,' Fiona said grimly.

'I would normally have received my dividends by now,' Mrs Barnet went on, 'but Mr Parker happened to find a wonderful new opportunity recently and let me in on the ground floor, so to speak.

'He re-invested my money there, at a much higher rate of interest, which is wonderful for people like myself who are more or less on a fixed income.

'The colonel did his best to leave me well provided for, of course, but even he couldn't have foreseen how dreadfully the cost of living would go up in just a few short years.'

'I'm sure he couldn't,' Fiona murmured.

By now she was even more suspicious of Aaron's motives. Was he involved in scamming pensioners? It was one thing to try to protect the inheritance he expected to get from his uncle — unlovely though such behaviour might be, but far worse to be stealing from members of the public, if indeed that was what he was up to. She pretended not to understand what Mrs Barnet was saying.

'So you've lost out on your dividends this time around, then?'

'Oh, no, dear. They've just been deferred for the moment. No pain, no gain, as they say.'

'But why didn't Mr Parker wait until the interest was due and just reinvest the capital then?'

Mrs Barnet looked bewildered. 'I'm not sure. I suppose he ploughed everything back in. That way I'll get more in the end.'

Fiona was no financial whiz, but even she knew that investments which promise high returns were probably not rock solid.

'Oh, well,' she said at last. 'I'm sure everything is in order. I expect you have papers to explain all this, don't you.'

She could tell by the expression on Mrs Barnet's face that this was not the case, and her heart sank.

Having e-mailed Aaron Parker, Jeremy came up with a plan of attack. He hated telling lies, but he felt that some play acting was in order if he was to get to the bottom of what was going on. At the very least the man was trying to pressure his great uncle into doing something he didn't want to do, but Jeremy suspected that Jason Greaves might be only one player in a larger scheme.

Aaron responded immediately, and they set up an appointment in a café near the newspaper office. There was no suggestion of meeting at Palmerston Magna, but as Jeremy had already discovered, there was no office there. This of course wasn't significant in itself when many people worked out of their homes, yet it did suggest that Money Works was a small operation.

'We've met before, haven't we?' was Aaron's first greeting. 'You were with my friend, Ms Flint.'

'That's right,' Jeremy said easily. 'We worked together at one time, until Fiona decided to freelance.'

Aaron treated him to a long, assessing look. 'You're a newspaper reporter, then.'

Steady on, Jeremy told himself. Don't let him think he's being investigated. 'Yes, that's right.'

'You must be well paid, then, if you have enough spare cash lying around to need a financial adviser.'

'I had an aunt,' Jeremy said, mentally crossing his fingers to negate the lie. 'Aunt Martha, a dear old soul. I was always the blue-eyed boy, so when she died she left me all her money. Quite a lot of it, actually.'

'Quite so, quite so.'

'I don't know much about stocks and shares and so on, but the banks are paying so little now that I want to find something that results in a higher return. Much higher, actually.'

A cat sizing up a mouse might well be wearing a similar expression on its face, Jeremy thought, watching Aaron closely. The man was almost licking his lips.

'Er, how much are we talking about, Mr Dean? If you can give me a round figure I'll get to work at once to see what's available.'

'Yes, well,' Jeremy said. 'You must understand that I'm checking out more than one source. I notice on your website that you have several testimonials from satisfied clients. Would you mind very much if I speak to some of them before I make up my mind?'

Aaron's expression hardened, but he waved one hand in Jeremy's direction, palm up, as if to tell him to go ahead . . .

'Then I'll need addresses or phone numbers, please. All you show is a town or city.'

'Of course. Client confidentiality, you know.'

'Then how am I supposed to contact them?'

'Write letters to them, Mr Dean, and I'll make sure they are forwarded to the right people. Naturally, it will be up to them if they choose to respond.'

Jeremy felt as if they were engaged in some sort of shadow boxing, both making moves but not getting anywhere. He pretended to go along with this idiotic suggestion, although Aaron must think he was a simpleton to believe that his letters would go anywhere other than straight into the shredder.

He went right back to the office and looked up the Money Works website again. Were any of these testimonials genuine? E. Black, Bournemouth and F. Lowe, Hastings, could be anybody or nobody. One name did catch his attention, that of a Mr P. Pettapiece, of Bognor. There couldn't be many people of that name in Bognor, if the man existed at all.

Once again the internet came to his aid as he looked for entries in the Bognor telephone directory. There was indeed a listing for a Peter Pettapiece, so after making sure that Mr Kemp had gone to lunch, he picked up the phone and punched in the numbers. A woman answered, sounding harassed.

'If you're selling something, I don't want it. I've had three of you people after me today already and if I don't get my washing out in the next half hour it'll be too late to get it dry today.'

'I'm not selling anything,' Jeremy assured her, 'and this is a long distance call, so I mustn't keep you. I'd like to speak to Mr Peter Pettapiece, if he's at home, please.'

'Well, you can't then, can you? He's working on the oil rigs and he's away till the end of the month.'

'Oh, dear. Then perhaps you can help? I'm thinking of investing money with a firm called Money Works, and I understand that your husband is already a client of theirs. I was wondering if he'd recommend them?'

'Oh, I see. It's Dad you want. My father-in-law, Philip Pettapiece. He's down at his allotment at the moment, but if you like to call back after six, he'll be in by then. Be prepared to get your ears bent back, though. He's none too pleased with them Money Works people, that I can tell you.'

Gathering up his notebook and tape recorder he hurried off to the library, hoping to find Fiona there. She smiled when she noticed him hovering in the doorway and his heart lifted. Her attitude seemed to be softening towards him. Was there hope for them yet?

'I've met with Parker,' he announced, speaking in a whisper in case they were overheard, although there was nobody else nearby, other than the librarian at her desk.

'I spun him a yarn about good old Aunt Martha dying and leaving me a bundle, which I now want to invest. That got him hooked, all right.'

'I didn't know you had an Aunt Martha!'

'I don't, but he's not to know that. The thing is, he was cagey about letting me speak to satisfied clients, but I managed to trace one anyway, thanks to the glories of modern technology. He wasn't home when I called, but his daughter-in-law indicated that he's not thrilled with Money Works. I'll probably find out more when I get back to him later.'

'I've met with another of Aaron's customers, too. A Mrs Barnet, a new client of mine, as it happens. When we discussed my fees she explained that she couldn't pay me until her next dividend cheque arrives, and guess who her financial advisor is?'

'Our Mr Parker!'

'You've guessed it. Apparently her money didn't arrive on schedule because it's been reinvested at a much higher return. It sounds funny to me because she doesn't seem to have any forms confirming what's been done on her behalf. On one level she seems to trust him, but I sense that she feels uneasy underneath.'

'It looks as though he wants to avoid leaving a paper trail,' Jeremy nodded, 'but it beats me how anyone would hand over their money without insisting on some proof of where it's gone and what the broker is supposed to do with it.'

'Perhaps that's why he likes to deal with older people, then, hoping they won't ask too many questions. You hear of so many seniors being taken in by con men, and they can't all be senile, can they? Most are probably like me, people who were brought up to trust professionals such as doctors and police-men. If I had money to invest, I'm not sure how I'd go about it on my own.'

'He seemed keen enough to get his greasy paws on Auntie's cash,' Jeremy sniffed. 'I hope he doesn't see me as a pushover.'

'It might be better if he does, don't you think? We don't want to alert him until we've got proof as to what he's up to.'

Jeremy shrugged. 'Speaking of which, have you heard from him lately? You're not seriously thinking of breaking into Jason's house with him, are you? I've got enough to do without visiting you in jail with a file hidden inside a fruit cake.'

'Don't be silly! Of course I'm not going inside that house without permission.'

'Then what do you propose to do when you get there? Have an argument on the doorstep about how your conscience is pricking you at the last moment, and you can't go in?'

'I shan't have to do anything of the sort. Aaron has a key, but what he doesn't know is that Myrtle had the locks changed. When he discovers that his key doesn't work, all I have to do is look amazed and say I can't understand it. Meanwhile, it's up to you to get the evidence we need and then we take it to the police.'

'Whereupon he lands you in it as his accomplice.'

'His word against mine,' Fiona said blithely. 'With Myrtle and Mr Greaves backing me up, Aaron won't have a leg to stand on.'

9

Philip Pettapiece had plenty to say for himself when Jeremy finally managed to get in touch. 'It's my feeling that this Parker chap is an out and out crook,' he said, bellowing into the phone so that Jeremy was obliged to hold the receiver away from his ear. 'You're some sort of reporter, you say. I hope you're going to write a stinging expose so he can't con others the way he tried to con me!'

'First of all I have to get proof, Mr Pettapiece. If I make accusations in print with nothing to back them up, the paper could get sued.'

There was a long silence.

'Are you still there, Mr Pettapiece?'

'Yes, lad, I'm still here. Just putting my thoughts in order. All right, then, here we go.' Jeremy held his little tape recorder close to the phone so as to record the story.

'Years ago, I bought an insurance policy, you see? Not one of those things that pays out after you're dead; that wouldn't do me much good, would it? The idea was that you paid in so much a week for years and some time down the road it would come to maturity, giving you a lump sum for your retirement. Back then I had fancy ideas about visiting America some day, or buying a boat and sailing away into the sunset, and that's what I was saving up for.'

'Sounds like a good idea.'

'Ay, well, I'm older and wiser now, or so I thought, and I have other things to do with my time. Money has lost its value over the years and what seemed like a real windfall when I started out isn't worth a hill of potatoes now. My friend, Charlie, he has the allotment next to mine, he tells me I should reinvest it somehow, make some real money, so that's what I did.'

'And you placed it in the care of Aaron Parker, I suppose,' Jeremy said.

'How did you happen to come across this Money Works place, Mr Pettapiece?'

The older man cleared his throat. He explained that his friend Charlie was responsible. 'Just leave it all to him, he said. Old Charlie had a computer, see his family gave it him for Christmas. He took a course at the recreation centre and after that there was no stopping him. Always looking things up on the internet, he was.'

'So you invested your money with Parker, and then what?'

'It seemed all right at first, and then my dividends never arrived. I got Charlie to send Parker an email and he wrote back to say I could have the interest if I liked, but he'd come across this wonderful new opportunity and wanted me to plough everything back in to this new scheme. Told me it paid 15% interest. Well, I may be old, but I'm not stupid. Nobody is paying that sort of interest these days.'

'I've heard a similar story from someone else in Marston,' Jeremy interrupted, thinking of Fiona's new client, Mrs Barnet.

'I daresay he's trying it out on all sorts of people, lad. I said no thanks, I'm sticking with the original scheme, and if he didn't like it I'd just draw my money out and leave it at that. Oh, no, he said. There were penalties for taking it out early; he didn't want me to do that.'

'So you've never seen your dividends at all?'

'Oh, yes, he's a clever one, is that Mr Parker. Three days later he shows up at my annual home with a cheque in his hand. Not my capital, you understand, just the annual dividend I'd been promised in the first place.'

Jeremy was disappointed to hear this, and said so.

'Just you hold on, lad, until you've heard this next bit. I want you to sign this paper, Mr Pettapiece, he says. It's to protect your investment, he says. Well, my old dad always warned me never to sign anything without reading it through first. Once your signature is on that paper, our Phil, they've got you where they want you, he says. Well, this paper said I was giving Parker my power of attorney!'

'What!' Jeremy was horrified. 'Once you'd signed that it would mean he had the right to do anything with your money, or your belongings, anything!'

'Exactly. I may not be an educated man, but I do read the newspapers and I know what a power of attorney is, and I asked him what he thought he was playing at.

'You've got me all wrong, Mr Pettapiece, he says. This protects you or your loved ones if you should have a stroke or be unconscious as the result of an accident. I'd be able to handle your money in case of trouble on the stock market and save you from losing the lot. The market can be very volatile at times, you know.'

Having heard this he had no doubt now that Aaron had tried the same trick with Jason Greaves, except that Jason was too astute a man to fall for it. It was even possible that harming him was a way of achieving that end. Had he been to the hospital, hoping to get a signature while the poor man was still groggy from his injuries?

'So naturally you informed the police?' he asked now.

'I told Parker I was going to contact them, but he only laughed at me. This conversation never took place, he said. I did tell our Peter's wife what was going on, and she did call in at the police station, but it didn't do any good.'

'They didn't believe her?'

'Oh, I expect they believed her, all right, but they said that so far no crime had been committed. That's where he was cunning, you see. Giving me that cheque meant he'd kept his part of the bargain, at least for the moment. Of course, I can kiss goodbye to my little nest egg. He'll find some way to make that disappear. Well, we live and learn, don't we? Live and learn.'

This conversation made Jeremy more

determined than ever to foil Aaron Parker. There was something particularly evil about a man who would try to separate old folks from their savings.

What had started as a kindness, meant to help Fiona protect Mr Greaves, had now turned into something of a crusade for Jeremy Dean.

Fiona dropped in to visit Myrtle and her house guest. She was pleased and surprised to find them looking very lively indeed. Even Jason seemed to be sparkling with enthusiasm over something. As long as she had known him there had been a lingering sadness in his eyes, which she had attributed to his missing his late wife, Muriel.

'We've got something to tell you,' Myrtle sang. 'In fact, you'll be the first to know. We're getting married!' Standing at her shoulder, Jason grinned from ear to ear.

'How lovely!' Fiona cried. 'Congratulations! I'll hope you'll have many happy years together. When did all this happen?'

Mr Greaves seemed happy to let his future wife do all the talking, so Myrtle went on to say that they had made their decision the previous evening and that the announcement would be in this week's Chronicle, and then the whole world would know. 'Of course, I have to phone my children today and let them know. It wouldn't do for them, to find out from somebody else.'

'I'm thrilled for you both.' Fiona was half inclined to say that as Myrtle had been angling for this for some time it was no surprise to her, but perhaps it was best to say nothing. Myrtle might well be letting Jason believe this was all his idea!

'When is the wedding to be?'

'Oh, quite soon, I should think. There's no point in hanging about, not at our age.'

'And you'll live here, in this house?'

'No, we mean to sell both our houses and buy somewhere new, perhaps one of those flats meant for retired people.

'The money we get from the sale of

the two houses will enable us to buy somewhere really nice, with something left over for a rainy day. It's going to be such fun, like starting out all over again. It makes me feel quite young!' She bustled off to put the kettle on, leaving Fiona and Mr Greaves staring at each other.

'Now we'll have to add a new chapter to your life story books,' Fiona remarked, when Myrtle returned, staggering under the weight of a tray, laden with good things to eat. 'I hope you plan to have pictures taken at the wedding. That can be the final one in both your books, the bride and groom going off into the sunset together.'

'I don't know about the sunset,' Myrtle laughed, 'but I hope we'll be able to manage a weekend somewhere nice. We haven't really discussed that yet. What I want to know is, have you and that nice young man of yours made it up yet? Perhaps we could have a double wedding!'

Mr Greaves looked aghast, and

Myrtle was quick to reassure him. 'That was a joke, dear. We're talking about my big day! I've no wish to be upstaged by a beautiful bride half a century younger than myself! I do hope we'll be hearing more wedding bells in the near future, though.'

'I'm afraid not,' Fiona said sadly. As she said that she realised that she had forgiven Jeremy for elbowing her out of her job. It hadn't been his fault completely, but in her dismay at the time she hadn't been willing to admit that. The sad thing was that while they had been meeting to confer over this Aaron Parker business they had slipped into their old easy companionship yet seemed unable to take the relationship a step farther.

The old chemistry was still there, but somehow they could not bring themselves to bridge the gap. Jeremy was probably wary of putting a foot wrong and Fiona herself had been too hurt to be able to trust again too soon.

She came down to earth with a start,

realising that Myrtle was saying some-thing. 'We might never have got together again if it hadn't been for you, Fiona, so I'd like you to be my bridesmaid, dear. How about it?'

Fiona was overwhelmed. 'I'd be honoured, of course, but wouldn't you rather have one of your daughters?'

'I think not. If I chose one and not the other there'd be hurt feelings, and we want a quiet wedding. It won't be the sort of do where the bride swans down the aisle with several bridesmaids, and then there'd be a fight between my little granddaughters, vying for the role of flowergirl. No, two attendants will be quite enough.'

'Who will be best man?' Fiona wondered, turning to Mr Greaves. 'One of your friends from the club?' Aaron was his only male relative; heaven forbid that he should be chosen to support the groom on his day of days!

'What about that chap of yours?' he said gruffly. 'This Jeremy I've heard so much about. It should be somebody your own age. You can't be matched up with some old codger the age of your grandfather.'

'I'll certainly ask him,' she promised. Unseen by her, the older couple exchanged gleeful looks.

Fiona was walking home, feeling cheerful. It was wonderful to think that she had brought these two kindly people together. The phone was ringing as she came through the door and she raced to snatch it up. She felt a sick feeling in the pit of her stomach when she realised who was on the other end of the line.

'Aaron Parker here, reminding you of your promise to come to Uncle's house with me. We can go this afternoon, if you're free.'

How had she ever got herself into this mess? Fiona cast around for some reasonable excuse to turn him down, and came up with nothing. If she refused to go, he'd only come after her again, and how was she ever to get the proof they needed to put the man behind bars?

'Hello? Are you still there?'

'Um, I was just thinking. Wouldn't it be better to go after dark?' She was stalling for time. One way or the other she wasn't about to cross that doorstep. If she could persuade him to go in alone perhaps she could call the police, saying she'd seen an intruder go inside. No, that wouldn't do, either. He'd probably tell them she was acting as his look-out.

'No, it wouldn't. It would be a nuisance to have to search the place using torches, and we might have to put the lights on. Some nosy neighbour who knows that Uncle is in the hospital would be sure to see them and wonder what was going on. Now, are you coming with me, or not?'

'Yes, I'll come,' she said, hoping he didn't notice her reluctance.

When she arrived at Mr Greaves' house some time later Aaron was standing beside his car, his fingers drumming impatiently on the bonnet.

'You took your time,' he grumbled.

'I came as soon as I could, and anyway, somebody was bound to notice your car sitting here while you were inside. Why didn't you leave it in the next street?'

'Because I want it to look as if we're supposed to be here. The neighbours probably know us by sight now, considering how many times we've been here in the past.'

Wordlessly she followed him to the front door, trembling with anxiety while he tried to fit his key into the lock.

'Oh, no. What's the matter with the thing? It won't go all the way in. It must have got bent or something.' He frowned at the key and then at Fiona. 'I suppose you don't have one, do you?'

She shook her head. 'No, I don't. There's no reason why Mr Greaves should have given me one. I always come here to interview him, or to go over photographs with him, so what would have been the purpose of my coming here when he wasn't home?'

Aaron tried the key again, but it still wouldn't work, and he gave a yelp of exasperation.

'Can I be of assistance?' The proverbial nosey neighbour had arrived, and was standing at Fiona's elbow, looking expectant. Fiona said nothing. Let Aaron weasel his way out of this one!

'You don't happen to have a spare key, do you, madam? I'm Mr Parker, Mr Greaves' nephew. He's asked me to collect some papers for him, but something seems to be wrong with this key.'

The woman looked him up and down, a steely glint in her eye. She was a stout woman with greying brown hair set in a badly done home perm.

'It's funny he didn't give you the right key, then!'

Aaron stared at the key in his hand, looking puzzled. The woman tossed her head and continued her tirade.

'He's had the locks changed, hasn't he? And I'm not surprised, after what happened. Some person broke in here and laid him out with a tyre iron. Leastways, that's what I heard. When I say broke, I mean he was inside where he didn't ought to be, though they say he got hold of the spare key from under the mat. Well, I know the locksmith came, because I saw his van sitting right there where you've parked your car. Ezra McDougall, locksmith, it said, right on the side of the van.'

'Yes, of course Uncle told me that,' Aaron said, smooth as silk. 'I expect he gave me the wrong key by mistake. Easy to do, of course. The poor old boy isn't at all well. In fact, I doubt he'll ever be the same again, after what's happened to him. Never mind, he'll have me to look after him from now on.'

'Oh, he won't be needing you,' the woman told him, her eyes gleaming with malice. 'He'll have that new wife to take care of him, won't he?'

'Wife? What wife?' Aaron's jaw dropped.

'Why, he's getting married again, isn't he? Surely you knew?'

'It's the first I've heard of it,' Aaron said, through gritted teeth. 'You must have made a mistake.'

'There's no mistake about it! My niece works in the classified ads department at The Chronicle and she dropped in this morning on her way to work. 'Whatever do you think, Auntie?' she said, 'You know that neighbour of yours, him who got bopped over the head the other day, well, he's getting married. There's been a notice handed in, to go in this week's paper.' Well, you could have knocked me down with a feather!'

'We'd better leave this for another time, Aaron,' Fiona mumbled, wanting to get away from the woman before she dropped any more bombshells. But it was too late.

'Get in the car, Fiona!' he snapped. 'We'll go straight over to the hospital and get the proper key from uncle.'

'Oh, but he's not in the hospital, is he?' the helpful neighbour explained. 'They let him out two days ago. I trudged all the way up there carrying a bunch of grapes only to find him gone. I do think somebody might have let me know. I had to eat them myself so as not to let them go to waste, but that was a mistake. Grapes always play havoc with my digestion. I said to my hubby, I said . . . '

But Fiona was never to know what hubby had learned, because Aaron grasped her painfully under the elbow and steered her to the car.

'I suppose you knew all about this!' he snapped, as he started the car and drove off with the gears clashing.

'I haven't been to the house or to the hospital for days,' she bleated. 'I've spent most of my time in the library. You'd be surprised at how often your uncle was mentioned in the press in the old days. He was quite an athlete, you know.' She was aware that she was babbling but was determined not to tell him where Mr Greaves was staying.

'We'll go to the hospital, and if they know what's good for them they'll tell me where he's gone. They must, I'm his next of kin.'

'Not for long, apparently.' The words slipped out before she could stop them, and he glared at her. She knew what he was thinking. Once Jason and Myrtle were married they would probably make wills in favour of each other, leaving Aaron out in the cold. Even if that didn't happen immediately, Myrtle could still make some claim on the estate as his wife, if she happened to outlive her new spouse.

'I'm sorry, I've forgotten that I promised to meet with my new client,' she blurted, when the car came to a stop at a red light. I'll talk to you later, Aaron.' She slipped out of the car before he could stop her, thankful that it wasn't equipped with power door locks.

Aaron shouted something she didn't catch, but the light changed to green and he was forced to move on because of the long line of vehicles drawn up behind. On the other side of the street a bus was drawn up, and, ignoring the abuse of impatient motorists she darted across the street and leapt on to the platform just as it moved away.

10

Out of the corner of her eye, Fiona saw a police station. Once again she was tempted to dive off the bus and go and tell her story there. But once again that would do no good. The police would only say that no crime had been committed so there was nothing for them to investigate.

A moment later the bus lurched to a stop. In keeping with everyone else, Fiona craned her neck to see what was happening. They had just arrived at a busy four-way intersection and it appeared that there had been an accident of some sort. Horns were blaring, pedestrians were hurrying to the scene and general chaos prevailed. The bus driver leaned out of the window and asked a passerby what was going on.

'Kiddie knocked off his bike by a car,

mate. He doesn't look badly hurt, but they've called an ambulance and the cops don't want the scene disturbed, as they put it. Looks like traffic will be snarled for a bit.'

'You heard that,' the bus driver said. 'Any of you wants to get off and walk, now's your chance. Can't give you no refunds, though. Sorry!'

Fiona pushed her way to the front and got off. Dashing on to a side street she managed to get away from the muddle, hoping that she wouldn't get into trouble later for leaving the scene of an accident.

It wasn't as if they'd seen anything; the bus had been too far away when the child came to grief.

She arrived at home, breathless and dishevelled.

'Mum? Are you there?' No answer. Madge had obviously gone out. Fiona grabbed up the phone, with her finger ready to punch in Jeremy's number at The Chronicle. Before she could act the phone rang shrilly. 'Please don't let it be

Aaron,' she begged.

'Hello?'

'Oh, Fiona, thank goodness I've caught you!'

Fiona hardly recognised Myrtle's voice, it was so shaky.

'Myrtle? Is that you? Is anything wrong?'

'Just listen, Fiona. I haven't got long,' her friend whispered.

'Aaron's here, and he means business. He came pounding at the door, demanding to be let in, and when I wouldn't answer he bawled at us through the letter box. Now he's trying to find another way in and I'm so frightened, Fiona. I tried calling 999 but I couldn't get through, just got a busy signal. Perhaps I dialled the wrong number or something. Can you come?'

'I'll be there as soon as I can.' Fiona promised. 'Just stay calm, and don't on any account let him in.'

'I've just heard the sound of smashing glass!' Myrtle wailed. 'He must have broken the pane in the back door and reached in to pull back the bolt.'

At that point the phone went dead. 'Hello? Hello?' But there was only the dial tone to be heard. Her mind whirling, Fiona hung up and then tried Jeremy's number.

'We've got to get over to Myrtle's house. Aaron has just broken in, and she's out of her wits with fear.'

'I'm on my way, Fiona. Phone the cops and then wait for me outside. I'll pick you up and you can show me where she lives.'

Keeping the story as brief as possible, Fiona gave Myrtle's address to the calm voice at the other end of the phone, saying only that an intruder had burst in on two elderly people, one of whom had already been the victim of an assault just days before. This done, she went out to the kerb and waited.

Jeremy's car came barrelling round the corner and skidded to a halt beside her. She jumped in, pulling the door shut as he sped off again.

He was exceeding the speed limit by

a good few miles per hour, but if the police happened to stop him that might be all to the good, given the circumstances.

'We'll go to the back door,' Fiona panted, when they arrived at the house in a cloud of dust. 'Apparently that's the way he broke in, so we shouldn't have any trouble doing the same thing.'

A nasty sight met their eyes when they burst into the sitting-room. Mr Greaves was cowering in an armchair, nursing one arm in his other hand. Myrtle was seated upright on a wooden chair, with a defiant look on her face. Aaron Parker was at her side, holding a vicious-looking spanner in one hand.

'Take one step farther and I'll let her have it,' he snarled.

'Are you all right, Myrtle? Has he hurt you?' Fiona tried to reach her, but stepped back as Aaron made a threatening gesture towards her friend.

'It would take more than a piece of scum like this to upset me,' Myrtle muttered, curling her lip at Aaron. As she spoke, they heard the sound of sirens approaching.

'Here come the cavalry,' Jeremy said cheerfully, heading for the front door to let the police in.

Aaron evidently realised when he was well off, for instead of using Myrtle as a hostage he stood meekly by, dropping his weapon as instructed by the police.

'I feel such a fool,' Mr Greaves quavered. 'That young puppy threatened to hurt Myrtle if I didn't sign some papers as he wanted me to. That's when I saw red. I tried to fight him off but he was too strong for me. A fine husband I'll make, if I can't even protect my wife from danger.'

'Don't be silly,' Myrtle told him. 'You were very brave, Jason, and as you can see, I'm not hurt at all. He expected you to cave in, but you didn't. I don't suppose he'd have done anything to me, really. He's a coward and a bully, that's all.'

Fiona and Jeremy exchanged glances. Aaron had certainly hurt his uncle before, enough to put the poor old chap in hospital for days. He would have had no compunction about a repeat performance.

* * *

Aaron was led away in handcuffs, mouthing insults. Fiona and Jeremy were asked to present themselves at the police station to give statements and the older couple were driven to the hospital to see a doctor. The worst was over.

'Thank goodness that's all over!' Myrtle sighed, when they were all back in her comfortable house. 'This wasn't exactly how I meant my life story to end!' Mr Greaves' arm had been put in a sling in Casualty, and she had been prescribed a sedative which she had refused to take.

'That young doctor didn't look more than fifteen or sixteen,' she explained. 'I'm not even sure if he was qualified.'

'Oh, I'm sure he was.' Fiona laughed. 'They wouldn't let him loose on the patients if he wasn't.'

'I expect you're right, but I didn't want a sedative anyway. We're the generation that faced Hitler, I told him. It would take more than an idiot like Aaron Parker to frighten me.'

Despite her brave words she looked quite pale, and there were dark circles under her eyes. Fiona felt she had to do something to help. Explanations could wait for another day.

'I want the pair of you to stay where you are,' she commanded, 'and I'll make you something to eat.'

She went into the kitchen and began to bustle about, putting plates in the oven to warm, and putting sliced bread in the toaster. Jeremy had followed her out.

'I didn't know you were so handy in the kitchen.' He grinned. 'You can make a meal for me any time.'

'Haven't you heard of women's lib?' she countered, opening the fridge and removing a carton of eggs. 'It's up to you to make a meal for me!'

'Fair enough! I'm a dab hand at opening a can of beans. Seeing as we're here, though, I'm happy to settle for some of your scrambled eggs. I'll return the favour another time.'

'Oh, no, you don't!' Fiona retorted. 'That pair in there are shocked and exhausted. They've had as much as they can take for one day. I'm off as soon as I've cleared up after them here and if you're wise you'll do the same.'

Jeremy hesitated. 'If we're not going to eat here, how would you feel about coming out for a meal? My treat.' He brightened considerably when she agreed to join him.

Over a meal in an Italian restaurant, they discussed their recent adventures, thankful that Aaron Parker was now safely locked up in police custody.

'What do you suppose will happen to him now?' Fiona wondered.

'I hope he'll go down for a good long stretch,' Jeremy answered. 'That all depends on what the police investigation turns up.'

'I hope they throw the book at him! Fraud, intimidation, bodily harm; surely that's enough to be going on with?'

'Intimidation, yes. We're witness to that, as far as this latest incident goes. I'm not sure about the rest, though.'

'Come on, Jeremy! What about the time Aaron hit poor Mr Greaves hard enough to send him to hospital? He's lucky enough to be alive, if you ask me.'

'Unfortunately Mr Greaves wasn't able to identify his attacker. All he could say was that the man seemed to be about the same shape and size as Aaron, but because of the disguise, and the fact that everything happened so quickly he couldn't swear to anything.'

Fiona twirled spaghetti around her fork in an expert manner. Jeremy wasn't so lucky. He swore when a morsel of pasta fell in his lap, leaving a tomato sauce stain on his clean jeans.

'More fool you for not putting your napkin over your trousers,' Fiona told him. 'Perhaps once they've investigated Aaron's business practices with his various investors they'll be able to put two and two together.'

Jeremy was too busy dabbing at his jeans with the corner of his napkin, which he'd dipped into his water glass, to answer right away.

Finally he looked up and remarked that it all depended on exactly what Aaron had been up to. 'There are several possibilities.' He checked them off on his fingers.

'One, he may have lost all his clients' money by mismanagement, say by investing in dicey stocks, or not pulling out in time when the market took a down turn. That may be bad news for them, but not something he can be prosecuted for. Two, he may have got greedy and used their cash for his own ends, meaning to replace it in due course, and them none the wiser. Then something went wrong and he was left out on a limb.'

'That sounds more like it,' Fiona mused. 'Mrs Barnet indicated that her dividends are overdue, and your Mr

Pettapiece was almost conned into giving Aaron carte blanche to deal with his money. I'm sure there must be many other investors with similar stories.'

'The police will look into that. Once they get access to Aaron's computer files they'll have a more complete picture.'

'What I don't understand is why he went after Mr Greaves the way he did. Was it because they were family? Perhaps he banked on the fact that if his fraudulent behaviour was uncovered his great uncle probably wouldn't press charges, for his niece's sake.

'And, horrible as it seems, I bet he felt he had a right to the money because it would come to him anyway, when Mr Greaves died.' A nasty thought struck her. 'Oh, Jeremy! You don't suppose he meant to kill him so as to get his inheritance sooner rather than later?'

'I doubt it. Aaron Parker is a nasty piece of work, but he doesn't strike me as a murderer. No, I think the original attack on Mr Greaves wasn't meant to happen. As the old boy says, he came home unexpectedly and surprised the intruder in the act of searching his house. Aaron probably panicked and had to fight his way out.

'And having been frightened off then, he still wanted to get control of Mr Greaves' private papers, which was where I came in, or didn't, as the case may be! I was supposed to be his cover.

'The neighbours had seen me coming and going, and perhaps knew about Mr Greaves having his life story recorded, so they'd think nothing of it when I turned up again. All I had to say was that he'd asked me to collect a few things he needed in hospital, and nobody would suspect a thing.'

'Only a nosey neighbour showed up and spilled the beans. Aaron knew he had to get hold of Mr Greaves' money before he married Mrs Siddons, and he needed to act fast. Unless the engagement announcement spelled out when the wedding was to take place, the happy couple could be tripping off to the registrar's office tomorrow, for all he knew.'

'It's not going to be in the registrar's office,' Fiona said. 'It's to be at St Mark's Church, where Myrtle is a faithful worshipper. So if you're going to be best man, you'll have to be on your the best behaviour.'

Jeremy's face was a picture of dismay. 'You don't mean I'll have to wear a monkey suit, do you?'

'That will be up to Mr Greaves,' Fiona said primly, although she already knew from Myrtle that an ordinary suit was all that was necessary. The talk then turned to the forthcoming marriage, and the couple's future plans. Fiona felt a little sad to think that she was sitting here with the love of her life, discussing someone else's wedding.

There was a time when she had hoped that she and Jeremy would have had such plans of their own, but that was then, and this was now. Wasn't it the poet, Robbie Burns, who said something about the best laid plans of mice and men? And he should know. If what she had read about him was correct, his love life had been full of problems and confusion.

The wedding was all that weddings should be. Myrtle Siddons, dressed in a silk suit in a beautiful shade of cornflower blue, with a flower-covered confection on her head, walked down the aisle accompanied by her son who was to give the bride away.

Fiona walked a few paces behind, stepping lightly in time to the music. She had a chaplet of rosebuds on her dark hair and wore a knee-length silk dress in rose pink, with a swirly skirt, and matching belt.

As Myrtle had promised, this was not a typical bridesmaid's dress, to be worn once and then put away out of sight, but an attractive garment that could be worn on other formal or semi-formal occasions.

Mr Greaves was waiting at the altar, looking distinguished in a dark blue suit, but Fiona had eyes only for Jeremy. Who would have thought he could look so handsome?

Used as she was to seeing him wearing jeans and a sweat shirt, with grubby trainers on his feet, she was amazed by the transformation. For one wild moment she let herself imagine that he was waiting at the altar for her, and they would shortly be making their vows.

Myrtle reached her place beside her bridegroom, the vicar stepped forward, and Fiona slid into the place which had been reserved for her in the front pew. 'Dearly beloved, we are gathered here . . . '

When the ceremony was over and the newlyweds had made their triumphant way down the aisle, the small congregation moved to the church hall, where the church ladies had prepared a delicious buffet.

'Your turn next!' Myrtle's daughter whispered in Fiona's ear as they lined up to fill their plates. Fiona murmured something noncommittal, but her heart was heavy.

Jeremy was having an animated conversation with a gorgeous girl who turned out to be Myrtle's granddaughter. It would be just her luck if this wedding proved to be the start of a relationship which would see Jeremy married off — but not to Fiona Flint!

'You haven't said where you're going for your honeymoon,' she said, turning to Myrtle so that Jeremy would be outside her line of vision. Myrtle beamed.

'Edinburgh. I've always wanted to see it, and so has Jason. It's steeped in history, which interests me, and of course there's so much more to it than that. People flock there from all over the world to see what it has to offer. We'll stay in a B & B and take gentle little jaunts around the city. It'll be a holiday to remember.'

'Edinburgh! How on earth are you going to get all the way up there?'

'By train, dear. Margaret is going to

drive us up to London, where we're booked into a hotel for tonight. We'll catch the train tomorrow. I'm looking forward to it so much.'

After the meal there was dancing. The wedding had taken place in the afternoon so this was quite appropriate. The music was provided by three men from Mr Greaves' golden age group, and somewhat to Fiona's surprise they were quite good, especially the one playing the trumpet.

Apart from Fiona, Jeremy and Myrtle's grandchildren, most of the guests were retired people, so most likely they preferred these slower dances, although at one point one couple did perform a lively exhibition to the tune of Hernando's Hideaway.

Fiona found herself drifting around the floor in Jeremy's arms, lost in a dream as the trio played Unchained Melody. She actually knew some of the words to that one and sang them under her breath as they moved in unison.

He touched her hair with his lips,

murmuring some endearment that she didn't quite catch. If only the dance could go on forever, she knew that she'd be the happiest woman in the world, but soon the last lingering notes faded away and the pianist stood up, smiling.

'Time for our break, ladies and gentlemen, but don't go away. Back in ten minutes.'

Myrtle sidled up to Fiona, removing the pretty corsage from her frock as she came. 'We're off now, then. I don't have a bouquet, but catch this!'

She hurled her flower at Fiona, who, taken by surprise, fumbled and missed it. Jeremy was quicker. Bending down, he managed to grasp it before it hit the floor and he held it up in triumph.

Myrtle beamed her approval. 'That means you'll be married within the year, young man, and no prizes for guessing who the lucky lady will be. Hey, Fiona?'

Jeremy needed no second bidding. He sank to his knees and gazed up at

Fiona. 'How about it, then?' He laughed. 'Will you do me the honour of becoming my wife?'

The onlookers cheered and clapped as Fiona, blushing furiously, gazed at him. 'Are you serious, Jeremy Dean?'

'Of course I'm serious, you idiot. Now, do I get an answer, or do I have to stay on this hard floor all night?'

When she shyly murmured yes he sprang to his feet and took her in his arms. It was hardly the most romantic proposal Fiona could have wished for, but what did that matter? They were together now, and this time nothing would ever come between them again. She returned his kiss fervently, not caring who saw them. Myrtle smiled softly and slipped away to find her husband.

We do hope that you have enjoyed reading this large print book.

Did you know that all of our titles are available for purchase?

We publish a wide range of high quality large print books including:
Romances, Mysteries, Classics
General Fiction
Non Fiction and Westerns

Special interest titles available in large print are:
The Little Oxford Dictionary
Music Book, Song Book
Hymn Book, Service Book

Also available from us courtesy of Oxford University Press:
Young Readers' Dictionary
(large print edition)
Young Readers' Thesaurus
(large print edition)

For further information or a free brochure, please contact us at:
Ulverscroft Large Print Books Ltd.,
The Green, Bradgate Road, Anstey,
Leicester, LE7 7FU, England.
Tel: (00 44) **0116 236 4325**
Fax: (00 44) **0116 234 0205**

Other titles in the
Linford Romance Library:

REBECCA'S REVENGE

Valerie Holmes

Rebecca Hind's life is thrown into turmoil when her brother mysteriously disappears and she cannot keep up rent payments for their humble cottage. Help is offered by Mr Paignton of Gorebeck Lodge, although Rebecca is reluctant to leave with him and his mysterious companion. However, faced with little choice and determined to survive, Rebecca takes the offered position at the Lodge — and enters a strange world where she finds hate and love living side by side . . .

HIDDEN PLACES

Chrissie Loveday

Young widow Lauren and her son Scott have emigrated to New Zealand, where they inherit an unusual home set in a thermal park. Lauren keeps the park running smoothly for tourists, but struggles with the huge task. Desperate for help, her advertisement for assistance is answered by hunky Travis, and she believes her problems are solved. But there are major troubles ahead and important decisions to be made. Both love and deception will play a part in her dramatic new life.

THE RESTLESS HEART

Kate Allan

Isabella Oakley is travelling to her relations who are to sponsor her for the London season, when her aunt is taken ill en route. However, she meets the attractive Anthony Davenport, and his scheming sister Pamela, who take Bella to London in their private coach. Then Bella encounters the mysterious Mr Montcalm, whom Anthony warns her away from. Yet Montcalm seems to be following her . . . Will Bella and Anthony overcome the machinations of his relatives and find love?

NOT QUITE A LADY

Angela Drake

Caroline Brooke is bereft when her father dies, leaving her his fortune. Whilst trying to cope with running her father's estate she attracts the interest of two admirers — sophisticated Edward Seymour and Robert Parker, a blunt-speaking mill master. Seymour offers her security in a world she knows and understands, whilst Parker challenges her long-held beliefs. But when she discovers a devastating secret, which threatens her heritage and reputation, how can she consider the attentions of either?